Praise for

Ride 'em Cowboys

J.P. Bowie creates a believable storyline with Ride 'Em
Cowboy... Ride 'Em Cowboy is a worthy read
~ *Fallen Angels Reviews*

Ride 'Em Again Cowboy adds erotic play with witty characters
to produce a story you will be happy you read
~ *Litrerary Nymphs Reviews*

...an unapologetic, sweet romance where everyone ends up
living happily-ever-after... ~ *Rainbow Reviews*

I0616944

Total-E-Bound Publishing books from
J.P. Bowie:

My Vampire and I

My Vampire and I
My Vampire Lover
Duet in Blood
Blood Resurrection

Ride Em Cowboy Collection

Ride Em Cowboy
Ride Em Again Cowboy

The Set up

Halloween Angel

Personal Trainers

The Officer and the Gentleman

Anthologies:

Fabulous Brits: Under the Law
Heatwave: Summer Bliss
Naughty Nooners: Lunches in Laguna
Christmas Spirits: A Present Christmas

RIDE 'EM COWBOYS
Collection

Ride 'em Cowboy

Ride 'em Again Cowboy

J.P. BOWIE

Ride 'Em Cowboys Collection
ISBN # 978-0-85715-062-2
©Copyright J.P. Bowie 2010
Cover Art by Lyn Taylor ©Copyright March 2010
Interior text design by Claire Siemaszkiewicz
Total-E-Bound Publishing

Published in 2010 by Total-E-Bound Publishing, Think Tank, Ruston Way, Lincoln, LN6 7FL, United Kingdom.

Total-E-Bound Publishing is an imprint of Total-E-Ntwined Limited.

Manufactured in the USA.

RIDE 'EM COWBOY

Dedication

My thanks to Michele for her sharp eye and guidance through the editing stages of this book, to Carol Lynne for her ongoing support – and of course for Phil, always.

Chapter One

"Yeehaaa!" The exultant cry from Parker Jones carried across the corral as the bronco beneath him bucked and pranced like coiled wire come to life.

Royce Chandler, leaning on the corral fence, one foot planted on the second rung, rolled his eyes and looked sideways at the man standing next to him.

"He just loves himself, doesn't he?" he remarked to the older man who stood steadily chewing on the plug of tobacco in his mouth.

Jim Ballard gave him a cursory glance. "He's pretty darned good though," he muttered. "Knows how to ride 'em."

He's pretty all right, Royce thought, feeling his cock twitch at the sight of Parker's perfectly round bottom bouncing up and down in front of him. *Too bad he's such a big-headed jerk...*

"Whoa!" Jim let out an involuntary cry as Parker was thrown into the air, his arms and legs revolving like a helicopter in distress. He landed with a sickening thud on the hard, beaten-down ground and didn't move. A couple of ranch hands dived in to stop the bronco's dervish-like dance.

"Shit," Royce muttered, feeling a flicker of alarm when he realised Parker wasn't getting up or even moving. Vaulting over the fence, he ran to where the cowboy lay flat on his back.

"Jones!" Kneeling by the cowboy's side, he jostled his shoulder. "Jones? You okay?"

"'Course I'm not okay, you idiot," came the reply. "I think my back's broken."

Jesus... Royce looked up at the other men who had gathered around. "Aldo, call 9-1-1. Get an ambulance out here."

As the young ranch hand ran to the house to make the call, Royce felt the pressure of his cell phone in his jeans' back pocket.

"Shit, what was I thinking?" he muttered, pulling it free and dialling 9-1-1.

Parker opened his eyes and squinted up at him. "Gotcha all in a dither, ain't I?"

Royce narrowed his eyes at the other man. "You better not be faking this, Jones."

The cowboy winced. "What? You want me to have a broken back?"

"No...of course not. Oh yes—" Royce directed his attention to the emergency operator. "We need an ambulance out at the Double 'R' Ranch. Man with an injured back..." He paused for a second. "Could be broken. Please hurry."

Royce became aware of the other men's shuffling movements around him. He looked up sharply. "You guys can get back to what you were doing. I'll stay here with Jones 'til the ambulance arrives."

With a certain amount of relief, the ranch hands dispersed. Standing around, looking at an injured man in pain was not one of their stronger points.

Royce looked down at Parker. "Hang in there," he said quietly. "It won't be long before the ambulance gets here."

"Hurts like the devil," Parker muttered. "Guess I was too darned cocky 'bout tamin' that colt."

Royce took his hand and squeezed it gently. The man's work-worn hand felt so good in his. "You'll be fine. You'll be up and riding him again before you know it."

"You're bein' awful nice to me." Parker gave Royce a lopsided grin. "I always figured you had no time for me."

"You're one of my father's employees, Jones," Royce said tersely, trying to ignore the effect Parker's blue-eyed stare had on him. "So, obviously I care about your well-being."

"Oh, that's all then?"

"Well..." Again, Royce found himself unsettled by Parker's gaze. "Well...yes...no...I mean...I hope you're back isn't broken, Parker...I mean, Jones—" He broke off as Parker squeezed his hand hard.

"Stop," Parker whispered. "I know what y'mean, Royce."

For a long moment, the two men remained immobile, gazing deeply into each other's eyes. Then Royce cleared his throat, removed his hand from Parker's grasp and stood up.

"Where the hell's that ambulance?' he muttered.

"Come with me," Parker said quietly from his prone position at Royce's feet.

"What?"

"Come with me, please. When they take me to the hospital, I want you there...with me."

Royce looked down at Parker, then knelt again by his side. "Okay," he whispered.

* * * *

Royce felt as though he'd been sitting in the waiting room all night. Glancing at his watch, he realised it had only been an hour. What was taking them so long, for Pete's sake? He just wanted to know Jones was going to be all right so he could go back to the ranch and tell his father not to worry. His dad always worried when one of his hands got hurt. He'd already called four times wanting an update.

"They haven't finished X-raying him yet, Dad," Royce had said over and over. "I'll call *you* when I have some news."

He looked up as a doctor approached him. "Mr. Chandler?"

"Yes. How is he?"

"Pretty good. Nothing's broken. Helps he's young and in such good shape, of course, but he's going to be in pain for some time, and we're going to keep him overnight for observation—just to make sure there's no internal bleeding. Are you a friend of his?"

"Uh…no. He works for my father."

"Oh. Well, he's asking to see you."

"He is?" Royce forced out a laugh. "Probably wants to know he still has a job."

Jeez, he thought, wincing. *Did that sound crass or what?*

"Yeah, I expect he does." The doctor gave him a cool look. "Well, why don't you go on in so you can put his mind at ease on that score? He's in room two-eleven."

Feeling like a jerk, Royce walked down the hall to Parker's room. He stood for a moment outside the door, then taking a deep breath, he pushed the door open and walked in.

"Hey…" Parker smiled at him from his hospital bed.

"Hey. Doc says you're in good shape. No broken bones." Royce approached the bed slowly. "How d'you feel?"

"Okay. Better now that you're here."

"Parker…" Royce didn't know what to say.

"Look, I know you think I'm a conceited jerk and all, and I guess when I saw you standin' there watchin' me, I kinda wanted to show off a bit — but what happened today made me think about things. You were so great the way you stayed with me. A lot of bosses would have had one of the guys do it. I just wanted to say thanks."

"You're welcome. I couldn't just leave you there."

Parker gazed up at him, and Royce gulped as he drank in every feature of the man's face. The curly black hair, tanned skin, the bluest, deeply set eyes with the little wrinkles at the corners when he smiled. And that mouth — those plump lips that Royce so wanted to kiss. He sat on the edge of the bed and tentatively reached for Parker's hand. Feeling the warm calloused fingers close around his, his breath caught in his chest, and almost as if in slow motion, he bowed his head towards Parker, brushing his lips lightly with his own. Parker's mouth opened slightly and the tip of his tongue ran gently over Royce's lips. Royce gasped at the sensation, then throwing caution to the winds, he slipped his arm under Parker's head, cradling him and crushing his mouth in an all-consuming kiss. As their kiss deepened, Royce's his cock hardened and the blood pounded in his head. Oh God, but he wanted to climb into bed with this man, hold his hard,

11

naked body in his arms, feel the scorching of his bare skin against his own —

"Oh…" Parker moaned against his lips. "That feels so great…but you're really fuckin' hurtin' me!"

"Oh, Jesus, I'm sorry!" Royce jumped back, letting Parker's head fall on the pillow, eliciting another deep groan.

"Shit! You tryin' to kill me, Boss?"

"Parker…God, I'm sorry. Did I break something?"

Parker chuckled. "No, but you're gonna have to wait 'til I get outta here before you get that rough."

Royce's face grew hot. God, what did he think he was doing? Kissing his father's foreman? What in hell was he thinking?

"Yeah…uh…Parker…I'd better go. You take care, okay?"

Parker watched him with sad eyes. "Sure, Boss. You take care, too."

"Right. I'll see you when you get back to work." He turned to leave then paused for a moment. "If you need anything, here's my cell number." He placed a card on the cabinet by the bed, then hurried from the room, closing the door quietly behind him.

He left the hospital, his mind in a whirl. As hard as he tried, he couldn't erase the feel and the taste of Parker's lips on his. It was just as well the guy was incapacitated, or he'd have been ripping off his clothes and climbing into that bed with him. Damn, but that cowboy was hot. Royce was hot, too, but his heat came from a sense of embarrassment and guilt at what he'd done.

Kissing Parker Jones — jeez, if word got 'round about that, his father would have a heart attack. It wasn't like

Parker hadn't wanted him, too. It was plain as day that he'd welcomed the kiss and wanted more.

Since Royce had come back home to the Double 'R' Ranch from law school, he'd been aware of Parker Jones. The man was so damned fine. Not tall, about five ten, but lean and hard muscled, and with an ass that had Royce's mouth watering from the get go. There wasn't a part of Parker that didn't enthralled him—except his goddamn attitude and ego. With a prickle of annoyance, Royce remembered how Parker had more or less snubbed him when he'd come around to meet all the ranch hands after he'd returned home.

Parker had made it obvious he didn't think a college grad was going to be of any real use on the ranch, and even though Royce had shown he could handle a horse and rope in a stray steer with ease, there had been no lessening of Parker's disdain. He'd supposedly muttered something to the effect that Royce wouldn't have a job on the ranch if it wasn't for his old man. Royce had wanted to confront him on that issue, but in the end, had decided to ignore it rather than give Jones the satisfaction of knowing he was pissed.

Still, the slur had rankled for some time. But Parker had seemed so different lying there tonight—so vulnerable. And that kiss...

Royce shook his head to clear his mind of that memory. *Forget it*, he told himself. *Nothing can come of it anyway...more's the pity.*

His cell jangled on the seat next to him, and he flipped it open. "Royce Chandler."

"Hey, Boss."

"Parker? You all right?"

"Yeah. Listen. 'Bout what happened—"

"Yeah, I know. *Shouldn't* have happened. I'm sorry about that."

"I'm not sorry. Felt nice."

Listening to Parker's low husky tones, Royce felt his cock harden inside his jeans. Parker's chuckle so close to his ear sent tingles all through him.

"Guess what, Boss?"

"What?"

"I've got a hard-on just thinkin' about you. Too bad you're not here to take care of it."

Royce groaned. "Parker…"

"It's okay. I know you think you made a mistake. I just wanted to let you know how great you made me feel. *Real* great."

Royce hesitated for a moment then said, "I really liked it too, but…"

"I know. It wouldn't do for you to hook up with the likes of me."

"No, believe me, that's not the reason." Royce bit his lower lip as he thought of what he had to say. "My dad doesn't know about me being gay. He'd have a stroke if he found out. My mom knew, but she made me swear I wouldn't tell him. It would kill him, she said." There was a long silence on the other end. "You still there, Parker?"

"Uh huh. You sure he doesn't know?"

"Yes, I'm sure. Why d'you ask?"

"Well, because he said somethin' to me one day…"

Royce tensed. "What did he say?" he asked through tight lips.

"He said you were the best son a man could ever have — even if, you'd probably never marry and give him a grandkid."

Royce was stunned. His father knew? Then why hadn't he…

Wait, could he really trust what Jones had just told him? "Parker, you're not lying to me are you?"

"'Course I'm not! I wouldn't lie about something like that. I know how important something like this is."

"And you, Parker?" Royce was hesitant. "How many know about you?"

"One or two of the guys. They're cool about it for the most part. They don't know 'bout you, though. And Royce…you know that thing I was supposed to have said about you when you came back from law school?"

"Yes. I wouldn't have a place on the ranch if it wasn't for my old man."

"Well, I never said that. I've never even thought it."

"But—"

"Yeah, I know someone told you that, but they were lyin'. I hope you believe me."

"Parker, I don't know what to say."

"Say you believe me."

"I believe you. But that first time I tried talking to you, you practically turned your back on me."

Parker chuckled. "That's because I was tryin' to hide the bulge in the front of my jeans."

"Oh…" Royce smiled and was silent for a beat or two, catching a vision of that bulge and feeling a tingle of excitement in his own groin. Clearing his throat, he asked, "How are you feeling? Still in pain?"

"Not so bad. I think you kissin' me made me forget all about the pain."

"I could come back…"

"Visitin' time's over. Maybe tomorrow?"

"I'll be there soon as I can."

"Thanks, Boss."

Royce heard the sound of a long, loud yawn.

"Shit," Parker continued. "They gave me somethin', and now I can't stay awake."

"That's good. I'll see you tomorrow. Sweet dreams, Parker."

"Only if I dream of you."

Smiling, Royce closed his phone. What a day, he reflected as he drove on to the ranch. If anyone had told him that Parker Jones and Royce Chandler were going to share a kiss while Parker was lying in a hospital bed, he'd have laughed in their face. And not just a kiss, but a desire to take it much, much further, and if it hadn't been for his being so darned pushy and forgetting Parker was actually in a hospital bed because he'd been hurt, who knows where it might have gone? Thinking back on that moment when their lips first touched, Royce could again feel the excitement that the kiss had brought him. Suddenly, he couldn't wait for tomorrow. Tomorrow they would have time to spend together, to talk, and to find out if what had passed between them was just a physical attraction or something much more.

* * * *

Royce watched his father stride from the corral to the barn and hoped when he was his dad's age he'd look as fit and spry. Everyone said Royce looked just like his dad did at his age, and he was happy about that. His mother had given him his blond hair and green eyes, but Aaron Chandler, his father, had bequeathed him his height and build.

"Royce, you goin' up to see young Parker today?"

"Yes, Dad, soon as I see the horses fed and groomed."

"Don't you worry about that, son. We'll have Bob or Aldo take care of them. I thought I'd come with you. See how he's doin'."

Royce felt an immediate twinge of disappointment. He really wanted to be alone with Parker so they could talk more—and yeah, kiss some more, too. Still, Parker was in the hospital. It wasn't the best place for a romantic exchange.

"That's good, Dad," he said. "He'll be glad to see you. We'll leave when you're ready."

"I'm ready now—oh hell, what does *she* want?" Aaron glared at the house where Annie, their housekeeper, waved frantically at him. She held her thumb and little finger to her ear, signalling he had a phone call.

"Be right back," he muttered, striding off towards the house.

Royce rounded up the two hands his father had mentioned and told them to take over in the stables, then he strolled slowly over to the house to wait for his father.

He hadn't been able to forget what Parker had told him the night before about what his father had intimated. How had his father found out? Royce didn't think his demeanour or body language had given him away. He'd always been careful to act the straight guy on the ranch. Maybe his mother had told his dad.

His thoughts were interrupted by his father yelling for him to come inside for a moment.

"Goddamn it, son. It's the bank on the line. There's a shareholder's meeting they forgot to tell me about—and I gotta attend. You go on to the hospital without me. Tell Parker I said hope he's doin' better. And tell him we need him back here soon as he's able."

With difficulty, Royce refrained from an unseemly jump for joy. "Okay, Dad. See you later." Whistling a jaunty tune, he headed for his Jeep. Fate sometimes sure had a way of taking care of things.

Chapter Two

Parker's face lit up with a smile as Royce knocked and entered the room.

"Hey, Boss."

"Parker." Royce held out the box of candies he'd picked up at the gift shop in the entry hall. "You look good."

"So do you." He took the candies, holding onto Royce's hand. "C'mere..." He pulled Royce down into a long, lingering kiss. Royce stroked Parker's unshaven cheek as they kissed then let his hand slip down to caress Parker's chest, rubbing his hand over the fine covering of dark hair and gently teasing his left nipple.

"Oh, jeez," Parker moaned against Royce's lips. "Feels so good."

"I can do better," Royce whispered.

"I bet you can. I can't wait to get outta here," He put his hand on the back of Royce's head and pulled him in for another kiss. Royce's tongue swept into Parker's mouth. The gentle kiss became forceful, demanding, and Parker was shaken by the almost electrifying jolts it created in every fibre of his body. His cock was so hard it ached, tenting the sheet and begging for release. Royce's hand slipped further south, and he gasped into Parker's mouth as he encountered the length of hard flesh that jutted upwards from Parker's crotch.

"Wow," Royce breathed. "So the rumours were true."

Parker blinked. "What rumours?'

"That you're hung like some of the horses you break." Royce smiled into Parker's eyes, and the cowboy tapped him lightly on the chin.

"You sayin' you can't handle it?" he asked, grinning.

"No, I'm saying I was lying about those rumours."

"Hey!" Parker gave him the evil eye. "It's way too soon to start insultin' me, you know."

Royce kissed him again. "I know. I was only teasing. I can't wait to get my lips around what you got down there."

"No time like the present."

The sound of heavy footsteps heading towards the room made Royce jump back from the bed with a guilty start, and Parker rolled onto his side to hide his erection. The door was pushed open, and a large woman charged into the room, clipboard in hand.

"Well," she boomed, eyeing Royce up and down and obviously liking what she saw. "We've a visitor, have we? I'm Nurse Rothschild." She extended her hand for Royce to shake.

"Royce Chandler," Parker muttered. "My boss."

"A pleasure," Royce murmured, giving the nurse a slow, sexy smile. Easily done since he was still feeling the sexual stimulus from kissing Parker.

"How nice of you to show interest in an employee," Rothschild simpered, then dragging herself from Royce's gaze, she smiled at Parker. "Good news. The doctor says you're good to go today. Just take it easy for a few more days." She smiled at Royce. "And I'm sure your boss will see to that. The doctor is arranging some therapy for you, but it'll be a couple of days before you'll be up for that."

"Well, that's great news," Royce said. "I'll wait 'til you're released and drive you back to the ranch."

"It'll be a couple of hours," the nurse said, frowning.

"No problem. I'll stay and keep him occupied."

Nurse Rothschild beamed at him. "What a wonderful employer you are. Very well, you boys have fun until I get back with the paperwork."

Royce walked the nurse to the door, then closed it behind her. He winked at Parker. "Does this thing lock?"

"No, darn it, but get over here anyway."

Royce hurried to Parker's side. "She did tell us to have fun," he murmured, sitting on the bed. He smiled into Parker's eyes, took his hand and kissed it gently. For a long moment, both men were quite still, the feeling that they were on the threshold of something momentous giving them pause.

"*Parker*," Royce whispered, his voice sounding strangely thick to his own ears.

"I know…" The cowboy placed his hand on Royce's cheek, gently stroking the smooth skin with his fingertips. "This is serious, isn't it?"

"Yes." Royce suddenly realised he was trembling. His hand shook as he smoothed back Parker's curls from his forehead. His eyes never wavered from Parker's as he lowered his head to take Parker's lips with his. Their eyes wide open, the kiss they shared was filled with desire and longing, and if there had been any fear in Royce's mind that this was perhaps no more than a fleeting, physical attraction, it was swept away by the rapture of Parker's kiss.

Oblivious to all else, it was no small miracle that they heard the approach of heavy feet outside the door. Just in time, Royce managed to sit back, leaving a respectable distance between himself and Parker as Nurse Rothschild entered the room flourishing Parker's release papers.

"Here we are," she said, all smiles. "Just sign here, Mr. Jones, and I'll let your friend here help you with your clothes." She handed Royce a plastic bag while still talking to Parker. "Those are painkillers to tide you over 'til you see your own doctor. Now, don't overdo things for a few days, and you should be just fine."

The two men smiled at the nurse as she turned to go. "Thank you Ma'am," Parker said, winking at Royce, then under his breath he muttered, "Let's get the hell out of here!"

* * * *

Royce glanced at his watch as he drove Parker towards the ranch. Almost noon. "I have an idea," he said.

Parker gave him a sideways look. "Am I gonna like it?"

"I hope so. There's a Day's End motel a few miles ahead. What if I get a room so you can rest up for a few hours?'

"Rest up?"

"Well, you know." Royce grinned at him. "Put your head down. That kind of thing."

Parker roughly rubbed Royce's thigh. "Sounds good to me — and you *are* the boss."

"And don't you forget it," Royce said, chuckling.

The room at the Day's End motel proved nicer than they had expected. The motel was mostly deserted, so Royce had asked for a room well away from the rest just so his "friend, who had just been released from hospital, could sleep peacefully for a few hours". The room was spacious and had a king-size bed and a party tub.

"How much extra did that thing cost you?" Parker asked, staring it.

"A whole ten dollars," Royce replied, grinning. "Of course, I was only thinking of the therapeutic aspects for you," he added.

"Considering what you're gonna put me through, I might just need it," Parker said, pulling Royce into his arms. He winced as the effort caused a pain to shoot through his spine.

"Take it easy," Royce murmured. "We *are* going to do this again, you know."

"I know. I just want to feel you pressed against me, bare skin to bare skin."

"Your wish is my command." Royce unbuttoned Parker's shirt, slipping it gently over his shoulders, then roughly removing his own and throwing it to one side.

"Oh," Parker groaned as Royce moved his chest lightly against his. "Feels so good."

"Yes." Royce's voice felt strangely thick to his ears. "Yes, it does." He inhaled Parker's scent—the musky maleness of leather and the outdoors that made his senses reel. Oh God, this is all he'd ever wanted, all he'd ever craved ever since seeing Parker for the first time. Parker in his arms, his lips a tantalising inch from his own.

"Royce," Parker whispered. "Have you any idea how many times I've dreamed of this moment? You and me, like this. I can't believe it's really happenin'."

Tears stung the back of Royce's eyes at Parkers' words. "Jesus, you're all I've wanted from the moment I first saw you."

"Well then..." Parker's smile tickled Royce's lips. "What say we stop all this yammerin', and get on with it?" His lips met Royce's in a scorching kiss. His tongue swept into Royce's mouth sending shock waves through him.

Oh, dear God. Royce almost wept with joy as the heat of his desire coursed through him, setting his groin on fire and his cock springing to attention, pushing against the firm barrier of his jeans. *Gotta get outta these clothes...*

Parker pulled at his belt and zipper, freeing his raging erection from its confinement. Jeans and boots were ripped off and tossed aside, then Parker knelt in front of him. Ah Jesus, his tongue licked him, tasting him.

Parker savoured the pool of pre-cum that poured from Royce's cock. Oh yeah. He slid his lips over the head, laving the underside with his tongue and loving the effect it had on Royce. Royce's hands caressed Parker's face, stroking his hair while he gasped with pleasure, thrusting his cock deep inside Parker's mouth.

Yeah, I want to fuck you, baby, Parker thought. *Fuck you deep and hard.* He cupped his hands about Royce's small round buttocks, pulling him in even deeper. He slipped his middle finger inside the moist cleft, pushing past the brief resistance, 'til his finger was all the way in, lightly caressing Royce's sweet spot. Royce's cock jumped in Parker's mouth, spilling more pre-cum over his tongue.

Royce bit down on his lower lip, visibly trying to overcome the tug of his orgasm deep inside him. He pulled his cock free of Parker's mouth and fell on his knees before him, holding him in a crushing embrace.

"Uh!" Parker winced from the pain.

"Oh shit, I'm sorry," Royce whispered, easing up, lying down on his back. "Here, lie on me, I'll take the weight. That's right. Feels nice."

Dammit! Parker cursed mentally. He'd wanted this to be perfect and here he was with a fucked up back, but Royce was right. It did feel nice. Way nice. Royce's body was a thing of beauty—soft smooth skin stretched over hard muscle.

God, but I so want to fuck you.

As if he had intuited Parker's need, Royce wound his legs around his waist and lifted his hips off the floor. Parker pushed forward, his hard cock thrusting between Royce's thighs.

"Wait up," Parker groaned. "We didn't come prepared."

Royce smiled up at him. "Yes, we did." He reached for his jeans and pulled a foil wrapper from the pocket. "There's a machine outside. Here," he said, ripping it open. "And it's lubed, too."

Ignoring the pain in his back, Parker slipped the condom over his raging erection. He hovered on all fours over Royce's willing body. His gaze swept over Royce's slim, sweet torso. He lowered his head until his lips could reach Royce's chest. He brushed each small, hard nipple, then teased them gently with his teeth. Royce squirmed beneath him.

"Fuck me, Parker. Let me feel your dick inside me. Fill me up."

Royce's pleas were like music to Parker's ears, making his cock grow even longer, harder, leaking into the condom as he positioned himself at the opening to Royce's core. A long shuddering breath escaped his lips as he eased himself into the tight hole. He paused as he saw Royce's eyes widen with the shock of his invasion, then encouraged by the wanton smile that immediately played on the young man's lips, he plunged further inside. Royce moaned, his hands reached for Parker's butt, holding onto him, pulling him deeper, his hips thrusting upward and taking every inch of the cowboy's long hot cock.

Parker grinned down at him. *Man, the little fucker was really enjoying this*, he thought He thrust forward, driving his dick into Royce, then he pulled back, almost all the way out, before plunging down again, causing Royce to gasp and whimper at the sensation.

"Oh yes, Parker," he cried out, his grip tightening on Parker's butt. "Fuck me!"

"Yeah," Parker grunted, slamming home again into Royce's slick, hot depths. "Yeah, you like that, Royce?"

"I love it," Royce panted. "I love *you*, Parker!"

Those words, inflamed with the passion that was surging through both men's bodies, brought Parker to the edge. His mouth found Royce's, claiming him with a kiss that seared them both with its intensity.

"Parker, Parker," Royce was mumbling into his mouth. Parker shut him up by pushing his tongue even deeper into his mouth. The rapture he felt almost eclipsed the pain in his back. Jesus, but he'd never felt like this before. He wanted to stay inside Royce forever, hold him forever, kiss him forever — never let him go.

Sweat from his brow spilled onto Royce's face as he gazed down into the other man's eyes. "You're mine...no one else's now, you understand? You're mine."

"Yes," Royce whispered, staring up at him with a kind of quiet adoration. "All yours."

Parker pressed forward, his engorged cock now begging for release. He groaned as his thrusts quickened, driven by the lust, and now the love, he felt for Royce. His breathing became harsh and laboured as his orgasm overtook him. Royce reached for him, dragging his face down to his own, his mouth covering him with hot, wet kisses. They climaxed together with cries torn from deep within them. As they clung to one another, their bodies writhing in their ecstasy, words of love tumbling from both their mouths, the realisation of what this now meant washed over them like a sensual, but comforting, flood.

Parker collapsed on top of Royce with a long satisfied sigh, his lips pressed to Royce's throat. He had never felt so spent, yet so fulfilled.

Royce's lips touched his cheek. "How do you feel?' he whispered.

"I need a back replacement," Parker said, smiling.

"Oh jeez, I'm sorry."

"Shut it." Parker squeezed him. "I feel terrific. You?"

Royce chuckled. "Like I've had a four-by-four shoved up my ass."

Parker frowned. "Sorry. Was I too rough?"

"Now, you shut it." Royce stroked Parker's face with his fingertips. "You were incredible. And what I said before, Parker, I really meant it. I love you." His breath shuddered as he gazed into Parker's eyes. "I know it might sound like I'm rushing this, but I've never been more sure of anything in my life, Parker."

"Love you, too," Parker said, his voice gruff with emotion. "If I ever doubted we'd be good together, I'm happy to be proved wrong."

"It was good, wasn't it?"

"Better than good." He sighed as he slipped out of Royce. "I *think* I can stand up."

"Maybe we should use some spa therapy on your back."

"Not a bad idea."

"Come on then. I'll start filling the tub." Royce helped him stand, then the two of them stood locked in each other's arms, unwilling to move.

"You feel so damned good in my arms," Parker whispered.

"Where I belong," Royce murmured kissing him lightly on the lips. "Except now, you gotta let me go, so I can run that hot water."

"'Kay, I guess." He watched Royce as he padded over to the big tub in the corner of the room. God, but that was the prettiest body he'd ever seen on a man—and without a doubt, the cutest ass any man had ever been blessed with. Just looking at those twin globes of plump flesh made him hard again.

Gingerly, he sat down on the edge of the bed. Man, his back hurt—but what the hell could he expect after what he'd just done to it? *And let's face it, Parker, you'd do it all again soon as the boy says he's ready for another go 'round.*

Maybe this time, though, they could do it on the bed.

Royce's smile, as he walked back to where Parker sat, was angelic. Who'd have thought he could be such a wild-man in the sack? Or on the floor, as it turned out. Royce sat beside him on the bed.

"You want me to fetch something to drink...beer, or something stronger maybe?"

"Beer sounds good."

"Okay. You go soak in the tub, and I'll rustle up a six-pack. Need some help getting in the tub?"

"I'll manage," Parker growled.

"You don't have to be Mr. Macho around me. I don't want you falling and hurting yourself again."

Parker looked at the concern in Royce's eyes and gave him a wry smile. "Okay…yes, I need a hand getting in the tub. But just this once, mind?"

Royce cupped Parker's face in his hands and kissed him sweetly. "Just this once," he murmured.

Parker groaned. "You keep doing that, and I'll need an ambulance to get outta here."

Chapter Three

After Royce left, Parker relaxed in the hot water, his back up against two of the jets that gently massaged and kneaded his muscles, bringing him a feeling of bliss. This, on top of what had just taken place between him and Royce, made Parker start to feel like life was worthwhile after all. Truth to tell, he'd been looking to leave the Double R for some time. When Royce had arrived, he'd started to have second thoughts. Royce's blond good looks and witchy green eyes had attracted Parker from the first moment he'd laid eyes on him. But when they hadn't exactly hit it off, he'd begun looking for the door again. But now...

He smiled as he remembered Royce's sweet wildness and the words of love that had spilled unfettered from him. Lying there, basking in the afterglow of what had taken place between them, Parker could almost envisage a life the two of them could share. Maybe they'd get their own spread somewhere. Hell, that would be something, wouldn't it? A horse ranch—maybe even one of those dude ranches, where the rich folks pretended to be cowboys for a weekend. He could just see Royce gettin' into that—sweet talkin' the ladies and convincing them they needed to make the ranch a home away from home. One look at that sweet ass of his and they'd be signing on the dotted line in no time flat.

His daydreaming was cut short as the door was flung open and Royce bounced into the room.

"Miss me?" Royce asked as he deposited two large brown paper sacks on the table.

"You bet I did."

"I've had a hard-on ever since I left, just thinking about what we did." He started to shuck off his clothes. "Mind if I join you?"

"There's plenty room." Parker's eyes gleamed with lust as Royce eased his body into the tub.

"Mmm, feels good," Royce murmured, leaning close to kiss his cowboy's mouth. "How's your back?"

"Good and ready for another go-around with you."

"That's what I wanted to hear." Royce scooted round and lay between Parker's legs, his back against Parker's chest. "Oh, wow," he murmured, feeling Parker's hard cock against his butt. "You *are* good and ready." His back arched sensually as he felt Parker's lips on his shoulders and the man's hands sliding down the sides of his torso, caressing the hard, lean muscles he found there.

"You feel so darned good," Parker said through a sigh of contentment, mingled with lust.

Royce took Parker's hands in his and held them pressed to his chest. "I was thinking about you and me…at the ranch. How are we going to do this? I mean see each other without causing some kind of talk? I don't want it to be a problem for you with the other guys."

"It won't," Parker said firmly. "If anyone gets in my face, I'll bounce 'em of the wall."

"That's what I mean. Dad won't like it if you get into fights with them."

"It won't come to that." Parker kissed the nape of Royce's neck. "It'll be fine, don't worry."

Royce shivered in his cowboy's arms and pressed his body harder against him. "Let's get out of the tub and onto that bed."

"Sounds like a plan."

Royce pushed himself to his feet, then held out his hand to help Parker up. As he did so, the water level in the tub went down, exposing the water jets, and sending a hard jet of water into the air, hitting Royce squarely on his butt crack.

"Yikes!" Royce yelped. "What the…?" Then he started to laugh as he reached for the off switch.

Without Royce's body to shield Parker from the water, it hit him in the crotch, almost knocking him over. "Shit!" he yelled.

Royce grabbed for him and the off switch at the same time.

"Oh, my balls," Parker groaned, steadying himself against the tiled wall.

"Poor Parker," Royce crooned, putting his arms around him. "Shall I kiss them better?"

"That might work," Parker said, trying to sound pitiful while hugging Royce to him at the same time.

"C'mon, let's dry off, and I'll make you feel like a new man," Royce teased. He stepped out of the tub and grabbed a white fluffy towel. Parker followed, and Royce wrapped the towel round him. He patted Parker's skin with the towel, all the while gazing into his eyes and laying little kisses on his lips.

Parker grew harder as he put his hands on Royce's hips, pulling him in closer. Royce's kisses travelled south, down over Parker's torso, teasing his nipples gently with his teeth before falling to his knees and bringing Parker's erection to his lips. He kissed the tip and probed the slit with his tongue, savouring the juice there. He looked up, smiling, as Parker groaned and gently stroked Royce's face with his calloused hands. Royce kissed and nuzzled the rough palm then turned his attention back to Parker's straining cock. He swept his tongue over the wet velvety head, then laved the underside, sending shock waves of delight through Parker's body.

Parker gazed down at the blond head that moved in rhythm between his legs. Just the sight of that alone was enough to make him come—forget the sensation of trying to control the urge to flood Royce's mouth with his semen. Jeez, but he loved this man. He wanted to hold him, be with him always…

Royce fingered the cleft between Parker's buttocks, making him writhe in sensory overload.

"Aw, Royce…Jesus…" He bent to pull Royce to his feet then yelped as a knife-like pain shot through his lower back, sending him to his knees. "Shit! Oh, man…"

"Parker?" Royce caught him in his arms and lowered him gently to the floor. "Oh damn, Parker, you're hurt again."

"No kiddin'. Fuck, but that hurts."

"If I help you, can you make it to the bed?"

"I'll try." Gritting his teeth, he let Royce ease him up into a sitting position. "So far, so good," he muttered, grimacing.

"Just a little farther," Royce whispered, his arms supporting Parker's back and shoulders. Groaning, Parker got to his feet and made the couple of steps to the bed. Royce helped him sit.

Parker felt as if he'd been hit by a Mack truck. "Shit, I'm sorry."

"Not your fault," Royce said, his lips close to Parker's ear. "If anything, I'm as much to blame. Here, let me get your pain medication." He fetched a glass of water and the vial of pills the nurse had given him. "Better take two." He watched as Parker swallowed them and drained the glass. He kissed Parker tenderly. "Any better?"

"Yeah, your kissin's improving all the time."

"Smart-ass. Here, lie down. Gently now…" Royce couldn't help but notice that even though Parker was obviously in dire pain, his erection hadn't abated one inch. "Just lay there, Parker," he murmured, kissing the other man's hard chest and stomach. He leaned over and took Parker's cock in his mouth. As he sucked, his hands stroked and caressed the firm muscles of Parker's torso, bringing a long groan of pleasure from the cowboy's lips. Parker ran his fingers through Royce's thick blond hair, wanting above all else for the pain to go away so he could pleasure Royce as he was pleasuring him. But, oh that felt good. Royce's lips and tongue laving his hard flesh. Felt so good.

"Oh, yeah…" The words caught in a sigh seemed to spur Royce on, and the pressure of his lips brought Parker to the brink. "Mmm…Oh, God, Royce…Oh my God…I'm comin'." He tried to pull away, but Royce held him captive as he erupted with a shout of elation. Royce gagged as the hot semen shot into his throat, then he swallowed. He held Parker there until every last drop was wrung from him.

"Beautiful," he murmured, licking the head of Parker's cock. "You are so beautiful."

"Get up here," Parker growled. "I can't get down there, so you'll have to get up here so I can return the favour."

Royce scooted up so that his lips met Parker's. "No need today, baby," he said, smiling. "I'm going to let you rest now, so you get better fast—then, watch out!"

"But—"

"No buts. Just relax. We've got all the time in the world to make up for it."

"But—"

"Hey, I'm the boss, remember?"

"*Bossy*, more like," Parker said.

"Think you could sleep for a while? Those pills should make you drowsy."

"Shouldn't we be getting back to the ranch?"

"I'd like you to wait 'til the pain dies down some."

"Okay, *Boss*." He stroked Royce's cheek gently. "I guess I could doze a while."

Royce waited until he was sure Parker was sound asleep before calling his father.

"Where in hell are you?" the older man yelled. "I called the hospital. They said Parker was discharged hours ago!"

"We stopped for lunch, and he didn't feel so good, so I got a room at the Day's End." It was only half a lie, he thought. "He's asleep right now, but we should be back by dinnertime."

"Oh, okay. Bring him by the house. I've had Annie fix up the guest room for him 'til he's back on his feet."

"You did?"

"Can't have him fending for himself, can we? He's gonna have to take it easy for a few days."

"Right." Royce glanced at his sleeping buddy and winced. Just what had they been thinking? "Okay, Dad. We'll see you in a few."

"Okay, son. Look after Parker."

Look after Parker. Royce smiled as he closed his cell phone. He'd like to do that for the rest of his days.

* * * *

He let Parker sleep for about an hour then gently woke him up. "Hey, Cowboy." He laid a sweet kiss on Parker's lips. "Rise and shine. We have to hit the road. I called my dad," he said as Parker sat up, moving carefully. "He said you're going to stay at the house for a few days, 'til you're on your feet."

"I'll just be in the way —"

"In whose way?"

"Well, your dad's. Yours. Annie's. Everybody's!"

"Shut up, Parker. You won't be in anyone's way. Besides," he added with a mischievous leer. "Your room's next to mine, so I'll be able to watch over you night and day."

Parker looked shocked. "Not with your daddy in the house, you won't!"

"What? Afraid he'll railroad you out of town?"

"At the very least."

"Don't worry. I'll come with you." He kissed Parker's nose. "You don't get rid of me that easily."

Parker caught him by the nape of his neck. "No way I want rid of you." Their lips met in a scorching kiss, and both men felt the heat of desire rise in their blood. It

36

would have been so easy to just give in to their lust for one another, but Royce knew Parker needed a break from all this physical activity.

He pulled back from Parker's arms, panting slightly. "No you don't," he teased. "Come on. I have to get you home. Get dressed before I forget my good intentions and ravish you again."

Parker grinned at him. "In that case, I might never get dressed again."

* * * *

They were quiet on the trip back to the ranch, due mostly to the fact Parker slept most of the way. Those pills were mighty strong, Royce thought, but he was glad Parker was out of pain for the time being. Missing the sound of his voice, Royce contented himself by stroking the inside of Parker's thigh and imagining what it was going to be like making love to him once his back had healed. He had an idea it might just border on the sensational.

He shook Parker gently as he drove through the gates of the Double 'R'. "We're home, Cowboy. Time to rise and shine."

Parker turned to look at him, a gleam Royce recognised in his eyes.

"Save whatever you're thinking for later," Royce murmured, pulling up outside the house. "There's my dad, and he's carrying a shotgun!"

"*What?*"

"Oh, sorry. It's a broom. He must've been sweeping the back patio."

Parker chuckled. "You'll owe me for that one!"

Royce smiled as his father threw the broom aside and strode towards them. "Parker, you need some help getting indoors?"

"No sir. I can manage, and there's no need to put yourself out having me stay here. I'll be just fine over in the bunkhouse."

"Wouldn't hear of it, son." Aaron Chandler held out a helping hand as Parker crawled out of the car. "I can see you're still in pain." He threw an anxious look at Royce. "You sure the docs said it was okay for him to leave? He looks like he's been through hell and back."

Royce's conscience gave him a nasty tweak. Maybe what they'd done in the motel room, wonderful as it had been, hadn't been the most sensible thing, considering Parker's condition.

"Yes, dad." He cleared his throat as he spoke. "They said he'd be fine. Just needs a couple days bed rest then some physical therapy."

Parker groaned as he stood and straightened his back. "Couple more of those pills might come in handy."

Royce nodded. "I'll bring them to you once we get you settled."

"I've set up a bed in the den, so you won't have to climb the stairs, Parker," Aaron said, taking his arm. "Lean on me, son. You sure look like hell."

Royce exchanged a look of longing with Parker as Aaron led him into the house. *Downstairs*, he thought. How could he get down there to visit Parker without the whole house hearing him creeping down those creaky old stairs? Even if what Parker had said was right—about his dad knowing he was gay—he doubted if he would go as far as okaying their having sex with Annie, their housekeeper, and himself in the house. Royce followed them inside, disappointment clouding his mind. After what he had experienced with Parker, it was going to be very hard to go about his business ignoring the physical need that already gnawed at him.

"I called Dr. Fishman," Aaron said, as he helped Parker sit on the edge of the bed in the den. "He's coming round in about a half hour. It will be good if he gives you a once over. You can never be too careful with back troubles."

Parker was immediately apologetic. "Gee, Mr. Chandler, you shouldn't have gone to all this trouble."

"No trouble, son. You're one of my best men. Gotta make sure you're back on the job lickety-split!" He patted Parker's shoulder to show he was joking. "Annie'll bring you some grub in after the doc's been here. Royce, why don't you go on over to the bunkhouse and get Parker's things?"

Royce looked at him dully. "What things?"

"His shavin' gear, PJ's, socks — those things!"

"Oh, right…"

"Don't wear PJ's," Parker mumbled.

Royce's eyes gleamed at the thought of a naked Parker wandering around the house.

"Uh, well…" Aaron cleared his throat. "With Annie in the house you'd best wear something. Royce, you got anything he can wear?"

"Yeah. I've got lounge pants and tees that should fit."

"Fine. Okay, Parker, you lie down and rest 'til the doc gets here. Anything you'd like?"

"Uh…some coffee maybe?"

"I'll tell Annie. Just relax now."

Aaron left Parker and Royce gazing across the room at one another. "Don't you go lookin' at me like that," Parker growled, a rueful smile on his face. "You've gotta behave yourself in your daddy's house."

"I know, I know," Royce said, closing the gap between them with three long strides. He cupped Parker's face in his hands and kissed his lips tenderly. "Keep that as a promise of better things to come," he murmured.

Parker took Royce's hands in his and kissed each palm. "I'm holding you to that promise," he whispered, looking up into Royce's eyes.

"I'll go get your gear. Is there anything you specially want?"

"Yeah…" Parker winked at him. "Somethin' I can't have right now. But failing that, there's a book I'm reading — *The Front Runner*. I'd like to finish it."

Royce smiled. "I read it a long time ago. You won't like the ending."

"I know how it ends. Not every story can have a happy ending, now can it?"

"Ours will, if I have anything to do with it." He bent his head and kissed Parker again. "Be right back."

* * * *

Parker had his own room in the bunkhouse, and as Royce stood looking around him at the spare but neat furnishings, the need for his cowboy to be there with him built with an almost overpowering force.

"Parker," he whispered, touching the patchwork quilt that covered the narrow bed in the corner of the room. He pulled back the quilt, and knelt, placing his face on the pillow, inhaling the unique scent of the man he loved. Before he quite knew what he was doing, he had stripped off his clothes and climbed into the bed, lying there, imagining himself wrapped in Parker's arms.

He reached down and felt his burgeoning erection. He held it in his hand, massaging it gently at first, then as the heat in his loins grew, pumping hard and fast.

"Oh, Parker…" His breath hissed out on the words. "God, but I love you so…" He bit down on his lower lip so hard he drew blood. "Oh…Parker…" He turned his face into the pillow as he felt his orgasm overtake him, breathing in again the faint traces of the scent he had come to love. His arm curled round the pillow, cradling it to him as though it were living flesh.

He moaned as he pictured Parker hovering over him, his strong arms about him, holding him pressed tight to his whipcord body. Royce's orgasm was explosive, sending streams of semen splashing over his chest and up under his chin. He drew a finger through the thick cream and placed it on the tip of his tongue. So this was what Parker had tasted when he'd lapped at his pre-cum. Not bad…but Parker's was sweeter.

When he returned to the house, the doctor was there, and Parker was standing stoically before him, his jeans slung around his hips, while Fishman, kneeling behind him, prodded and poked at his spine and pelvis.

"That hurt?" Fishman asked.

"Yep."

Another prodding. "And here?"

"Ow! Yep."

Royce sighed with impatience. "I think we can safely assume, Doctor, that Parker is in considerable pain. What we need to know is what can be done to help him get back on his feet."

Fishman threw Royce an irritated look. "What I can't understand is why the hospital released him," he said to Aaron, ignoring Royce. "I can't imagine that the ride home put his back out of whack like this. He should be in traction."

Parker and Royce exchanged guilty stares, and Royce felt like shit for making his friend a whole lot worse than he'd been. Even as he thought this, he couldn't help but feel rising lust as he gazed at Parker's naked chest, the dark hair that curled round his pecs, and the rosy nipples he'd feasted on earlier.

"Maybe we should call the hospital," his father said.

"No..." Fishman struggled to his feet. "If Parker promises to stay put in bed for a few days—and I mean stay put—no walking about for any reason, the muscles will relax and the inflammation should go down. They give you any anti-inflammatory pills?"

Parker nodded. "Can I start lying down right now?" he asked, wincing.

"Here," Royce leaped to his side. "I'll help you." He put his arm around Parker's shoulders and supported him as he lay back on the bed. Parker looked up at him and winked. Royce smiled then straightened up. "I'll go get those lounge pants and tees," he said, clearing his throat, and almost running from the room.

"I'll prescribe some stronger pills," Fishman said, looking at the vial Parker had brought from the hospital. "I'll stop in day after tomorrow and check up on you. Now, take it easy, Parker."

"Yes, Doc," Parker said mildly watching the doctor and Aaron leave the room. He looked up at the ceiling and heaved a long sigh. Shit, but this was a bummer. Served him right, he supposed, carrying on with Royce like that. Where the hell had his brain been? In his dick, that's where. Still, he'd do it all again — if only he could.

He smiled as Royce came in carrying his loungewear. "Whoa, fancy stuff," Parker exclaimed on seeing the CK label.

"Only the best for you," Royce whispered. "Let's get those jeans off you."

Parker chuckled. "That's my boy…one track minded."

"I wish," Royce muttered ruefully. "Lift your hips just a little, and I'll slide them off you."

Even that small effort caused Parker to wince in spite of himself. "Damn, but I'll be glad when this is all over," he said through gritted teeth.

"So will I." Royce folded the jeans, trying not to torture himself by looking at Parker's cock lying heavily on his left thigh. Sitting on the bed, he peeled off Parker's socks then covered him with the sheet. "I'll help you put the pants on later." He slipped the tee over Parker's head. "Can you put your arms through?"

"Yeah," Parker grunted. The job done, he lay back looking at Royce with affection. "I'm real sorry 'bout this, Royce. I'm gonna make this up to you, big time, when I'm back on my feet."

Royce was just about to kiss him, when he heard his father's footsteps in the hall. Thank God for wooden floors! He stood up as Aaron entered the den.

"So, all set? Annie will bring your supper in shortly." Aaron looked at Royce and shook his head. "Don't be so quick to bite off Doc Fishman's head, son. He's not a bad old quack."

"Yeah, sorry, Dad. I just figured he should know Parker was in pain without all that poking at him."

Aaron chuckled. "I'm a big believer in old-fashioned remedies myself. I'm betting a good belt of Old Tawny would make you feel like a million bucks, Parker."

"Uh, not on top of those pills, Dad."

"Maybe not. We'll save it for when you're recuperating."

"Sounds good," Parker replied.

"Okay, we're going to let you rest a while." He signalled that Royce should follow him. "I want to go over what them bank fellas had to say…"

Chapter Four

Royce's plan to have his supper with Parker was thwarted by Annie who shooed him away, saying he'd only make a mess trying to spoon feed the invalid, and she'd nursed a whole household of men what with being a wife, now widowed, and the mother of four boys. Aaron had chuckled at Royce's insulted expression.

"Come on, son. Let's you and me have a beer outside and Annie can vent to her nursin' ways. No point in arguing with her — or any woman for that matter."

Royce gave in and, beer in hand, followed his father outside to the back patio where they settled into the wicker armchairs Royce's mother had purchased only a year before she'd died. Aaron had never cared for the furniture, thinking it too flimsy for the outdoors, but since Hannah's passing he'd sooner die than get rid of it.

"It's good having you here, son," he said, his voice warm and sincere. He looked up at the star-laden sky before asking, "But what are your plans for the future? Since you worked so hard to get that law degree, I don't see you spending the rest of your days at the Double R."

"Funny you should say that, Dad." Royce stretched out his long legs in front of him as he relaxed into the cushioned comfort of the chair. "I've kinda taken a liking to this cushy life you have here." He grinned at his father as the older man raised his eyebrows. "Just kidding. I would like to spend more time here before making any decisions — if that's okay with you, of course."

"Of course it's all right with me, Royce. Stay as long as you want. I can always use a good hand here — and Parker's going to be out of commission for a while."

"Oh, I think he'll mend fast." *I hope to God he mends fast.* "He's tough as nails." *And I should know.* Royce grew hard inside his jeans.

"Yeah, your probably right," his father said. "Still, I don't want him overdoing it for a while. I know he wants to compete in the rodeo next month."

"Oh yeah? Which one?"

"Sacramento State Fair. He's already entered."

"Damn. I'm not going to miss that."

"Good. I was planning on attending, but the date clashes with another of those darned board meetings."

"Well, I'll definitely go — just to cheer on Parker."

Aaron grimaced. "If he's up to it."

* * * *

Before he went upstairs to his room, Royce looked in on Parker. "Hey, you didn't tell me you were competing in the Sacramento rodeo," he admonished.

Parker grinned up at him. "Well, we've only been on talkin' terms for about a day and a half — and most of that time we were kinda busy with other stuff."

"Right." Royce gave him a quick kiss on the lips. "You think you'll be ready for that?"

"I sure intend to be." He grabbed Royce's hand. "And for a whole lot more, before and after that!"

"Oh, Parker…" Royce's eyes misted looking down on his lover, as he now thought of him. My lover…it sounded good. "I'm gonna say a long and loud prayer tonight to get you better."

"Well…" Parker kissed Royce on his chin. "I sure can use all the help I can get."

"You sleepy?"

"Some. Hey, would you do me a favour?"

"Anything."

"I can't read lying flat on my back like this. Would you read me just a few lines of *The Front Runner*?"

"Sure."

"Annie saw it lying here and asked if she could read it after."

Royce chuckled. "And what did you tell her?"

"I said, yes. She's a woman of the world. One of her son's is gay, you know."

"No, I didn't know that."

"Yep…the youngest one. Cute as a button, too. Lives with his boyfriend in Santa Barbara."

"Wow." Royce picked up the book. "Where do I start?"

"At the bookmark."

"Oh right, duh." And so Royce read to him.

"I lost count of the times we made love that weekend. We were laying up treasures for the lonely months ahead."

Royce almost choked up on those words. Jesus, but he couldn't wait to start laying up treasures with Parker.

"You read so nice," Parker said, his blue eyes gleaming in the lamplight.

Royce placed the book on the table by the bed and bent to kiss Parker's lips. "Hurry and get well," he whispered.

Parker brushed his fingertips along Royce's jaw line. "For you, I'm gonna."

* * * *

One tortuous week later, Parker was on his feet and ready for the round of physical therapy both the hospital and Dr. Fishman had recommended. Royce would drive him into town to the clinic, then they planned to have lunch together before driving back to the ranch. They both looked forward to this — it would be the first time to be alone together since their sojourn in the motel. Even though there would be no stops at the Day's End, Parker knew just being alone with Royce would be enough — for the time being.

He looked out the window, and watched Royce striding across the yard. He looked so damned fine. Parker couldn't quite believe this handsome dude was his. His to hold, to kiss, to lose himself with, and to hear the words of love said over and over.

"Hey, you ready?" Royce's smile was enough to make Parker cream his pants.

"You bet — been ready for hours. Where've you been anyway?"

"Some of us have to work," Royce said smugly. "While others lay around pretendin' to be incapacitated old men."

"Huh...I'll make you eat those words one of these days."

Royce grinned at him. "Among other things."

"Don't go gettin' my hopes up, boy."

"Among other things!" Royce ducked as Parker swiped at his head. "Easy now, old man. Watch your back."

"Just you wait, Royce Chandler. Just you wait!"

* * * *

Royce looked up from the magazine he'd been reading while he'd waited for Parker. From the stunned expression on Parker's face as he walked back into the clinic's waiting room, either his first session with the physical therapist had gone really well or really bad.

"Man," he muttered. "That was amazing. That lady in there is a miracle worker."

Royce didn't mention the fact that he'd been very relieved to see the therapist was a woman and not some hunky guy with big muscles and white teeth—not that he was insecure or anything.

"That's great," he said, happily, guiding Parker towards the exit. "She say when you'll be fighting fit again?"

"Can't wait, can you?" Parker gloated. "Well, neither can I. She said I can go back to work after the next session with her."

"Terrific."

"Yeah, terrific. Means I can start training for the rodeo."

"And what else does it mean?" Royce teased.

"Dunno…maybe your dad has some new colts need breaking in… Ow!" Parker yelped as Royce squeezed his bicep, hard.

"You're obviously forgetting something much more important," Royce said, as they crossed the parking lot to his car. "It means that you and I can pick up where we left off, with you begging for my cock in your mouth, and the two of us all hot and sweaty and ready to fuck each other's brain out—that's what it means."

Parker smacked his backside. "You have a dirty mouth."

They grinned at one another as they settled into Royce's truck, and he started the engine. "Know what I was thinking?"

"I've got a fair notion."

"There's a spot down by the river I used to go to when I was a kid. It's kinda quiet...no one around. How about if we stop there for an hour or so? Just get some private time."

"You hear me arguing?"

Royce smiled happily. "Didn't think you would. I'm just glad you feel the way I do."

Parker stroked Royce's thigh. "You know I do..."

Royce pulled off the main road, steering his truck carefully over a bumpy and pot hole scarred dirt road that led down to the river, the banks of which were thickly lined with tall trees and bushes. He drove into the shelter of the trees, killed the engine, then leaned over to plant a hot wet kiss on Parker's mouth.

"I've missed this," he whispered, thrilling to the touch of Parker's lips on his.

"Me to." Parker pulled him in closer for another long deep kiss, their tongues meshing inside the moist heat of their mouths. Their desire for one another kicked in immediately, but Royce was careful not to give in to his impulse to dive onto Parker. He couldn't risk throwing his back out again.

"Let's get out of the truck," he muttered hoarsely. "I want to feel all of you pressed against me."

Parker got out of the truck as fast as he could, following Royce down through the trees to the river bank. His cock strained to get free of the denim that encased it. Lord, what that boy did to him. Just the sight of Royce's ass in his tight jeans as he bent low to duck under a tree branch was enough to fire him up. He grabbed Royce by his belt and pulled him into his arms.

"Damn, but you are beautiful," he breathed against Royce's lips. Their tongues tussled in each other's mouths, driven by their pent up passion for one another. In a millisecond, their shirts were off, their bare chests sliding together, their hands fumbling with each other's belts and button flies, while their mouths never lost contact, their lips swelling from the rough pressure they inflicted on one another.

Parker's calloused hand grasped Royce's cock, pulling it free of his fly, and pumping it hard. Royce fisted Parker's cock and for a time they remained, bodies and mouths locked together, bringing each other to the brink of orgasm.

"I want your cum in my mouth," Parker murmured and dropped to his knees, taking Royce's aching erection into his mouth.

"Ah...Parker," Royce moaned, fondling the cowboy's springy curls as he fucked his mouth with long smooth strokes. Parker pulled Royce's jeans down around his knees, then caressed his butt, letting his fingers stray between the cheeks, probing at the tight hole that longed for his attention. He released Royce's cock for a moment, coating his fingers with the saliva he'd worked up, then taking the hard flesh back into this mouth, he pushed his middle finger past Royce's resistance.

Royce groaned, and his dick jumped in Parker's mouth. "Mmm, yes, baby," Parker mumbled, his mouth full of cock. Royce's body shuddered, and as Parker squeezed his balls gently in his free hand, he let out a long, low guttural cry of sheer pleasure. His body bucked, sending his cock even deeper, and his hot semen flooded Parker's throat.

Parker rocked back on his heels, holding the head of Royce's cock between his lips so that he could taste the sweet saltiness of his lover's semen as it jetted into his mouth.

"Oh, jeez, Parker," Royce whimpered, his hips pushing forward, letting Parker take all of his cock back inside his mouth. After Parker had wrung every vestige of his seed from him, Royce slumped to the ground in front of his cowboy, his arms encircling him for support, his mouth seeking Parker's for the kiss he wanted more than life itself.

"Christ, but I love you, Parker."

They fell over on their sides, each one cradling the other, their lips and bodies pressed together, desperate that nothing should ever come between them. Parker's hands caressed and stroked the smooth skin that covered Royce's torso, feeling once again the deep desire that welled within him every time he was close to, or even thought of him.

"I love you too, Royce. God knows I love you. You've become everything to me, everything."

Royce stirred in Parker's arms. "Let me take care of you, baby." His lips travelled the length of Parker's torso, pausing to suck and nibble at both nipples, to tease the curly chest hair with his teeth. Parker held Royce's head between his hands, stroking the thick blond hair, caressing his cheeks. Royce breathed a long sigh of satisfaction as his lips found the prize he wanted more than anything else. Parker's cock—that long, thick shaft that sprang from his dark, curly pubic hair.

Royce took the head in his mouth, his tongue dancing over the rigid flesh while his hands kneaded the solid muscle of Parker's thighs. Parker groaned, letting himself give in to the sensuousness that swept through him at Royce's touch. He raised his hips, pushing against the pull of Royce's lips.

Oh, yeah…

Royce freed himself of his jeans then straddled Parker's hips, moving his butt sexily over Parker's cock. With his eyes fixed on Parker's, he slipped two fingers into his mouth, thoroughly lubricating them with his saliva, then pushed his fingers inside himself. Parker watched through half-closed eyes, his lips lifting in a small smile to match the mood of unbridled sensuality Royce was creating. Royce leaned down and brushed Parker's lips with his.

"Fuck me," he whispered. "Make me yours again, Cowboy."

Parker took the condom Royce handed him and rolled it over his rock-hard erection. Royce lifted his butt and guided Parker's cock inside him, slowly easing himself down on the hot, rigid length. Parker gasped as his cock was enclosed by Royce's heat.

"Oh…fuck, but that is too good," he murmured, holding Royce's hips and thrusting upward.

"Yeah, let me have it all." Royce's head fell back in his ecstasy, and Parker revelled in the sight of the long lean torso that hovered over him. His hands slid up over the warm smooth skin to reach for and tease the tiny nipples made harder by his touch. His passion and desire drove him into Royce with all the force he could bear. His hips lifted, bucked and thrust upward, ploughing into Royce with a fervour and need he had never felt before.

"Parker!" Royce's cry was filled with joy and wonder, and Parker couldn't control the sense of pride that filled his heart, knowing he was the one responsible for bringing Royce this rapture. They came together in great roiling spasms that amazed and exhilarated them with the emotional and physical intensity their orgasms had invoked. Royce's semen spattered over Parker's chest, his chin, and even found its way onto his hair. He collapsed over Parker with a long sigh of complete satisfaction.

"Oh, baby." His lips nuzzled Parker's ear. "You *are* the man."

"You ain't so bad yourself," Parker chuckled, kissing Royce's cheek and holding him pressed tightly against his body. "Phew, man...I never knew it could be this good."

"Even better than how I imagined it would be," Royce whispered. "I love you, Parker...*more* than love you. Is that possible? Is there another word for what I'm feeling?"

"Dunno...they say love is the greatest gift in the world. What could be greater than that?"

Royce kissed him slowly, savouring the taste of Parker's lips. He smiled into Parker's eyes. "Okay, I'll accept love – but only because I can't come up with a better word, right now."

They lay quietly in each other's arms, while overhead, the tall trees that lined the riverbank swayed in the gentle breeze that cooled the skin on their naked bodies. They moved even closer together for warmth, neither one willing to break the spell their lovemaking had cast over them.

Live for the now, Royce thought to himself. *Tomorrow can wait.*

Chapter Five

Three weeks later

The air was alive with excitement as Royce and Parker pulled into the parking lot outside the Sacramento Stadium. Everywhere, people spilled from cars, trucks and campers, setting up barbecues, kid's play areas, and generally having the time of their lives.

Royce went with Parker to the check-in station, wishing that he had enrolled for one of the competitions early enough to have taken part. If for nothing else, just to show his cowboy what he could do—apart from what he already knew, of course. Royce smiled to himself as he remembered the night before, and the one before that...and all the times they had made love, lying under star laden skies.

Royce followed Parker into the stadium, trying not to be too obvious about ogling his boyfriend's ass. But it was a beauty to behold, he thought, licking his lips. The hell with the rodeo—he couldn't wait 'til they were alone in the hotel room he'd booked for the night.

"Hey, Parker!"

The yell came from somewhere ahead of them, and Royce frowned as a young cowboy threw himself into Parker's arms, bear-hugging him and slapping his back with gusto.

"Drew, how the hell are you?"

Who the hell is Drew? Royce watched with discomfort as the two kibitzed for what seemed forever, until Parker turned to him, grinning from ear to ear.

"Royce, this is my old buddy, Drew. Drew, Royce is my boss at the Double R."

Drew held out his hand and touched the brim of his Stetson at the same time—a sign of respect for Parker's 'boss'. Royce took the extended hand in his, thinking, *so this is what I am – Parker's boss, not his lover or his boyfriend, nor even his friend…his boss.*

"Pleased to meet ya," Drew said.

"Likewise. You competing?" Silly question since Drew was in full wrangling gear, leather chaps and spurs.

"You bet." Drew's gap-toothed, sunny smile lit up his attractive face. He clapped Parker on the shoulder and pulled him close. "You and me, we'll kick ass as usual."

"So…" Royce watched as Drew swaggered off, the shape of his butt nicely outlined by his leather chaps. "You and Drew…?"

Parker sighed. "Yep…better get that out of the way right now so you won't be worried all day wonderin' about him and me."

"I didn't say I'd fester. I'm just curious, that's all."

Parker chuckled. "Yeah, right. Well, I met him at the gay rodeo in San Diego a couple of years back. We hit it off right away, y'know? He's a lot of fun."

I bet, Royce thought. "So, you were lovers?"

"Not really. Long distance and all. Drew's a professional. Lives in Texas. Only comes out this way for the rodeos. We kept in touch for a while, but then…well, you know how it is."

Royce tried not to think of Parker and Drew doing it, but in his mind's eye he could picture the two men, naked and sweaty, their arms around each other, while Parker ploughed Drew into oblivion. Strangely, this vision didn't make him jealous—just hard. The thought of watching Parker fuck another man was not something he figured he'd get off on—but now…

"Where the hell's that mind of yours now?" Parker asked, his eyes narrowing as he gazed at Royce.

"Uh…nowhere…I mean…" He adjusted himself as discreetly as he could. "I was just thinking…"

"I know what you were thinking, you little sex-pig, and it'll have to wait." Parker grabbed his arm. "Now, c'mon. I gotta get over there and sign up."

That afternoon, Parker showed everyone why he was one of the favourites at every rodeo he entered. Although Royce sat with his heart in his mouth, hoping his cowboy wouldn't have a repeat of his fall at the ranch, he couldn't help but be swept up by the excitement of the crowd that roared and cheered as Parker won event after event in the competition.

Parker hadn't told Royce he'd entered himself in the steer wrestling round. He'd guessed Royce would have made a fuss, and of course, he would have. It was the most dangerous event in the rodeo, and Royce had never seen Parker do this before. He sat with fists clenched tight, waiting for the steer to be released and Parker to spring through the gate.

Oh please, he anguished, his heart pounding in his chest. *Don't let him break anything or get gored.*

He was on his feet, yelling with the rest of them, jumping up and down with joy as Parker won a place in the semi-finals, his only major competition his buddy, Drew.

The last round was bareback — Drew out first. Royce was filled with admiration for the little cowboy as his bronco sprang into the centre of the ring, bucking like a crazy thing. Royce could see the tenacious expression on Drew's face as he rode out every effort of the bronco to unseat him. The roar of the crowd increased as Drew hung on until the animal beneath him in a wily move, stopped dead in its tracks, and Drew, taken unawares, flew over the bronco's head, landing flat on his back, while with a little snicker of triumph, the bronco trotted away. Drew, looking only slightly shaken, jumped to his feet, and waved to the cheering crowd.

"Ten seconds!" came the call. "That puts Drew McIntyre in first place!"

Now it was Parker's turn. *Ten seconds to beat,* Royce thought. *That's going to feel like an eternity on top of the beast that had been bred to make things as tough as possible for its rider.* Royce yelled Parker's name as he came charging out of the holding pen. His mount was a devil incarnate, twisting, turning, and leaping with all four feet off the ground. Royce couldn't imagine how anyone stayed astride the animal as it did everything but roll over on its side in an attempt to dislodge its rider. Royce wanted to look at the clock, but couldn't tear his eyes off Parker who clung tightly to the rigging — the only thing between him and being airborne, apart from the strength in his thighs.

Those thighs were going to get another workout later, Royce gloated.

A loud buzzer sounded telling the crowd Parker had exceeded the time needed for him to win. At any time, he could dismount and claim victory, but still he hung on, and Royce knew that he intended to break in the animal. The noise of the buzzer seemed to enrage the bronco, as it shook its head in frustration, its hind legs kicking so high its body was almost perpendicular to the ground. The crowd roared again as Parker remained firmly glued to the animal's sweating flanks. Then as if someone had pulled the plug, the bronco slowed and shook its head as if to say, "Okay, you're the man" and contented itself by trotting gently round the arena, head held high. The crowd went wild, and Royce's chest pumped with pride as Parker waved to him then blew him a kiss.

As they left the stadium Drew ran up alongside them, grabbing Parker's arm. "Wait up, Parker. I owe you a drink, remember? Wanna get together later? There's a party at the Downtown Sheraton, and I've got a room there."

Parker frowned. "Uh, well…Royce and I have plans."

"Well, I intended for Royce to join us," Drew said, sounding peeved. "That is, if your boss don't mind seeing you get fallin' down drunk, like last time."

"I don't mind," Royce said, a shade too quickly.

Parker shot him a glare then turned to Drew. "Okay. A couple of beers. What's the room number?"

"What?" Drew smirked. "You turnin' lightweight on us, Parker?"

"No," Parker drawled. "But, I really do not want my *boss* to see me fallin' down drunk in front of him. Might make him wonder about my self-respect and ability to do the job right."

Royce didn't miss the barb thrown his way, and he felt ashamed he'd jumped in so quick. He gave Parker a look of apology from under his long lashes.

Drew also seemed to get the point. "Well, shoot then. I'll see you guys about eight. Room two-twenty-five."

Parker was silent as he watched Drew swagger away with his slightly bow-legged gait, then he looked at Royce and sighed. "You know," he said slowly. "I've been lookin' forward to bein' alone with you ever since we planned this getaway. You might think me kinda anti-social, but choosin' between you and Drew—you win hands down. Now tell me, why were you so darned eager to go out drinkin' with him?"

Royce felt his face flush. "Well, no real reason," he mumbled.

"Because, if you were thinkin' for one minute that the three of us could get into some kinda *scene,* then you don't know me very well!"

"No, Parker..."

"Don't try to fool me." He unlocked the truck doors and climbed inside. He waited until Royce had settled in his seat, then he grabbed him by the arm. "I'm only going to say this once. I told you some time back that you were mine, and by that I meant I was yours, too—body and soul. As far as I'm concerned, there's no room for anyone else in our relationship. Now, if you've got different thoughts on this, then I'm the wrong man for you, and we'd better end it, here and now."

"Parker...no." Royce turned to him, an anguished expression on his face. "I'm sorry. It was the thought of you with him, *being* with him—it kinda turned me on.

That's all. Please don't be mad. I'd never cheat on you. Never!"

"Okay." Parker rubbed Royce's thigh roughly. "Just so we understand each other."

Royce relaxed a little, but then had to ask. "Why did you introduce me to Drew as your boss? Why not as your friend—or the boss's son, even? I'm not your boss, Parker."

Parker turned on the engine and pulled the truck into the exit lane before he answered.

"Parker?"

"Because I know Drew," he said finally. "I know if he got an inkling we were together, he'd set his sights on you—not that he hasn't anyway. I could see that look in his eye. He was lookin' at you as if you was naked."

Oh my god. Royce blinked with surprise. Parker was jealous, and to his shame, Royce felt himself becoming aroused by it.

"I can't believe it. You're jealous of your ex-boyfriend *maybe* wanting to get into my pants?"

"Don't joke," Parker growled. "Ain't no 'maybe' about it. Like I said, I know Drew."

Royce took Parker's hand and laid it in his lap, letting him feel his hardening cock. "There's only one man who gets to feel and see this," he said, unbuttoning his fly. He pulled his erection free and pushed it into Parker's hand.

Parker groaned. "What are you tryin' to do—cause a collision?"

"Yes," Royce whispered, leaning in to kiss Parker. "Your cock colliding with my ass."

Chapter Six

Drew sounded like he'd been expecting the call when Parker told him he and Royce couldn't make it for those beers after all.

"Well shoot, Parker…maybe next time, huh?"

"Yeah, Drew…maybe next time."

"If y'all change your minds, I'll be at the Cactus later tonight with some of the fellas."

"Okay, maybe see you there." Parker put the phone down, shaking his head. The Cactus? No way was he taking Royce there. That place was rough at the best of times, and after a rodeo, it would be insane.

Royce appeared, framed in the bathroom door, naked as nature intended, his taut body looking mighty tempting. "I'm taking a shower. Like to join me?"

"Don't need an engraved invitation for that," Parker said with a grin, pulling off his clothes, leaving them in a pile on the motel room floor.

"That's my boy." Royce opened his arms and wrapped them round Parker's warm, wiry body. Their kiss was hot and hungry, making both their cocks spring to attention.

Royce rubbed his against Parker's. "Mmm, baby. Feels so good."

"Shower," Parker growled, pushing him across the bathroom floor. "After what I've been doin' all day, hot water and soap's the only remedy."

Royce chuckled as he turned on the hot spray and pulled Parker into the shower with him. They embraced, standing under the hot spray, their hands sliding over each other's wet bodies. Royce took the soap from the shelf and lathered Parker's back, his soapy fingers lingering over Parker's muscular butt, running up and down the deep cleft between his buttocks. Parker pushed his crotch harder against Royce's, grasping both their cocks in his hand and pumping slowly, all the while keeping his lips locked on Royce's.

"Mmm," Royce murmured, breathing into Parker's mouth.

"Mmm is right," Parker said. "Turn around."

Now it was Parker's turn to rub the soap over Royce's sleek muscles. He kissed the nape of Royce's neck then ran his tongue down the length of Royce's spine. He knelt behind Royce, his hands parting the plump butt cheeks that were only a tantalising inch from his lips. He probed the pink hole with the tip of his tongue, then as this action wrenched a long low moan from Royce, he probed deeper, the musky smell and taste acting as an aphrodisiac, clouding his mind with lust.

"Oh, Jesus...Parker," Royce whimpered, arching his back, clutching at the sides of Parker's head, moving his butt in slow circles around Parker's thrusting tongue. This blissful sensation almost proved to be too much. Royce felt his orgasm build inside him. Too soon. He wanted this, but he wanted all of Parker inside him—every inch of that beautiful hard flesh.

As if he had intuited Royce's need, Parker stood slowly, his tongue now sliding up the length of Royce's spine. He tightened his arms around his lover's slim torso.

"Ooh, baby." Royce wriggled inside Parker's arms, pushing his butt into Parker's crotch. "What's that I feel knockin' at my door?"

"Ain't knockin. It's comin' in!"

"Oh…"

"Don't worry," Parker mumbled, and Royce turned to see the foil wrapper between his teeth. "I came prepared."

Royce chuckled. "I didn't know you were such a boy scout."

"Now you do…" Parker positioned his dick between Royce's butt cheeks and pushed slowly in. Royce bent over, supporting himself against the shower wall.

"Uh…yeah," he sighed, as Parker filled him with one long smooth stroke. "Oh, lover…you feel so good inside me." Once he felt Parker was all the way in, he stood, arching his back and leaning into Parker's body. He took his cowboy's hands in his and held them pressed tight against his chest. He smiled blissfully. Everything he wanted in life was right here, right now—Parker inside him, holding him, kissing him, moving rhythmically behind him, filling him with his love and desire. He exhaled a long sigh of happiness as he ground his butt into Parker's crotch.

"If I could stop time right now, I would," he murmured, turning his head to kiss Parker's lips. "I want to hold you inside me forever. Feels so wonderful."

Parker caressed Royce's face, keeping their lips pressed together. "Love you, Royce," he said when they came up for air. He grasped Royce's cock and pumped slowly in rhythm with the movement of his hips. Royce's head fell back against his shoulder and Parker nibbled at his earlobe. Royce moaned long and low as the rush of his imminent release built inside him.

"Parker," he gasped. "Oh, God…Parker." His body bucked and spasmed in the throes of his ecstasy, his hands clutching at Parker's body even as he felt his lover's throbbing cock erupt inside him. Parker started to yell as his orgasm overtook him, then clamped his mouth on Royce's shoulder to stifle the sounds of his elation.

"Oh shit…" Parker pressed his lips to Royce's shoulder where he'd bitten him. "Did I hurt you, baby?"

Royce chuckled and leaned backed against him. "Where, exactly?"

"Sorry, I bit you. I had to stop myself yelling like the horn-dog I am."

"Hey, a hickey's a nice reminder of what we did." He wriggled his butt, revelling in the feel of Parker's cock still inside him, still hard and hot.

* * * *

The four hour drive back to the Double R was uneventful apart from Royce wanting to stop just before they got there and spend time at 'their' spot by the river.

"Come on, Parker. Who knows when we can get time alone again? Dad's gonna have a heap of work for you, and I hate sneaking into the bunkhouse — we have to be so quiet, and you know how you like to yell when you come."

Parker groaned. "Royce, dammit, you are draining me dry."

"You're full of it." Royce chuckled as he realised what he'd said. "And I mean that, literally. No way you'll run dry in a million years." He stroked Parker's thigh sensually. "C'mon Parker, pretty please…"

"Oh, all right." Parker grinned at him. "You are the darnedest sex pig I've ever come across."

"How many have you come across, may I ask?"

"Hundreds…but you beat 'em all to heck!"

Royce laughed and squeezed Parker's hard thigh. "You saying I'm a nympho?"

"Somethin' like that…" He pulled off the highway onto the dirt road that led to the shelter of the trees lining the riverbank. Royce jumped out of the truck as soon as Parker had killed the engine.

"Let's go skinny-dippin'," he yelled, stripping off his shirt as he ran towards the river.

"You'll freeze that pretty ass of yours," Parker warned as he sprinted after him. "Water's colder than a witch's tit this time of year."

"Chicken!" Hesitating only long enough to shuck off his boots and jeans, Royce dived into the water, then came up spluttering, his teeth chattering.

"Told ya," Parker laughed.

"Told ya!" Royce mimicked, splashing cold water at Parker. "Get your butt in here. It's not that bad."

"By the looks of you turnin' blue it ain't good, either. I'll pass, thank you, and wait here, dreamin' of what you wanted to stop here for in the first place."

"You…" Royce stood up, sweeping the water from his blond hair. Parker gulped at the sight of him. That boy is so fine, he thought, his eyes raking over Royce's sleek, lithe torso, the wide shoulders and the sculpted muscles of his arms. Royce waded out of the water, holding his hands over his crotch. "Don't look at my dick," he mumbled. "I think it went into hiding."

"He'll come out soon," Parker murmured, pulling Royce's wet body into his arms. "I'll give him a hand."

"Mmm…" Royce snuggled into his embrace, and Parker cupped his bottom in both hands, pulling him in closer. "Love you, Parker," Royce sighed.

"Love you, too." Together, they lay on the springy grass, and Parker licked at the beads of water that had gathered on Royce's chest. Royce caressed Parker's face, and for a while they were content to simply lie there, holding one another, sharing soft, tender kisses. Then Parker's hand closed around the throbbing flesh that rose from Royce's crotch.

"See?" he whispered. "I told you he'd soon come on out."

* * * *

Aaron was happy to see them return, and even happier to hear how well Parker had done at the rodeo events.

"Damn, but I wish I could've been there," he complained, clapping his foreman on the shoulder. "Well done, Parker, well done. Annie's got your favourite meal in the oven—beef stew. We'll have the other hands over to celebrate. Royce, why don't you go tell them to clean up and be over at the house in an hour.

"Sure, Dad." Royce was still feeling the effects of the euphoria he always experienced after Parker had made love to him.

"Oh, by the way," his father added. "There's a letter for you on my desk. From some law firm in Los Angeles."

"Oh, yeah? I'll get it later. Thanks, Dad."

Aaron steered Parker indoors. "How about a shot to celebrate your big day? Still feel bad I couldn't make it there with you and Royce. You boys have fun?"

"Yeah." Parker was careful not to sound too happy about all the fun he and Royce had enjoyed. "We had a good time. Ran into some old friends. Y'know how it is. A small world in rodeo."

"Yeah." Aaron poured two shots of his favourite Old Tawny and handed Parker a glass. "I remember those days like it was yesterday. Well, here's to you Parker." They clinked glasses, then downed the liquor in one swallow. "Damn, but that's good stuff," Aaron croaked, wiping his mouth with the back of his hand. He reached for the bottle and poured them even more generous shots.

Hell, we'll be shit-faced before the other guys get here at this rate, Parker thought, knocking back only half his shot. *Better slow it down.*

"Whoa, Boss," he said chuckling. "Better wait for the others to get here."

They both turned at the sound of Royce's boots in the hall. "Hey, starting without me?"

"Just one, son… Here, get yourself a glass…"

"That's okay, I'm going to shower before supper."

"What happened to your jeans?" his dad asked. "Looks like you've been rolling on the grass."

He and Parker exchanged a quick but guilty look. "Oh, that…I slipped on something earlier. Must've been wet, I guess. See you in a few." With that he flew upstairs to shower and change out of the offending jeans.

* * * *

Dammit, Royce thought, pulling off his jeans. *Why didn't Parker noticed that big green stain on the denim? Most times he's looking at my ass anyway. You'd think he'd have said something.* As he stepped into the shower and began soaping himself, he thought of the time he and Parker had spent on the riverbank. *God, but that cowboy's hot. He just fills me up so well. But that's not all it is either. There's just something about Parker that makes me feel so darned good… so necessary…so in love.* He liked it that Parker was so possessive of him. "You're mine", he'd said — and he was right.

"I'm his," Royce murmured to himself. "And always will be."

When he got back downstairs, the living room was alive with good-natured talk and laughter. Jim, Ned, Bob and Aldo had all come up from the bunkhouse after cleaning themselves up and changing clothes. Annie was handing around homemade cheese pastries that went well with the beer they were all drinking. Old Tawny was used sparingly, it's effects widely known to be fairly lethal.

Royce helped himself to a drink from the bar. Scotch on the rocks being his drink of choice, then joined the others, sitting as close to Parker as he could without raising any eyebrows. The cowboy gave him a slightly tipsy grin, and Royce couldn't wait for the festivities to be over so he could sneak into the bunkhouse — even though he'd told Parker it wasn't really conducive to their making love — and forcing him into going down to the river. Well, not forcing exactly. Parker was always willing enough. Royce felt himself grow hard inside his jeans. *Shit, don't anybody ask me to stand up.*

"Royce…" His father beamed at him from his old armchair. "Give us a song, son — you know the one your

Mama liked so well. She loved those old show tunes," he added to no one in particular. "Annie'll play for you."

"Dad," Royce protested. "Not tonight."

"Hell." Parker nudged him. "I didn't know you could sing."

"He's got the voice of an angel," Annie declared proudly. "His mother and I used to love goin' to church to hear him." Royce groaned as she headed for the piano. "Come on, Royce darlin'. I think the one your daddy wants to hear is *Somewhere*."

"That's it, Annie," Aaron said, slurring slightly. "From *West Side Story*."

Blushing like mad, Royce stood and walked to where Annie sat playing an arpeggio as his introduction. Everyone in the room stared at him startled, as his clear tenor voice filled the room. *"There's a place for us, somewhere a place for us..."*

Royce tried not to look at Parker as he sang, but of course the words were all about them, weren't they? *"Hold my hand and we're halfway there, hold my hand and I'll take you there..."* As the final notes hung in the air, then quietly died away, there was a moment of total silence before the men all stomped, cheered and applauded. Royce blushed again and smiled, catching Parker's eye. He felt his breath stop in his chest as he saw the tears welling in Parker's eyes.

Oh please don't, he thought, *or I'll start really bawling*.

But it was his father who started bawling, resting his head in his hand while the tears slid down his cheeks.

"Oh, Dad..." Royce went to him. "Don't upset yourself."

"I'm sorry, son. You could've had a career—your Mama wanted it for you, but I was such a stubborn old bastard. No, I said...not show business for my son."

"Oh, stop your blabbing Aaron Chandler!" Annie poked him on the shoulder. "You're drunk that's what it is. Royce don't hold no grudges, do you, boy?"

"Of course not," Royce said, rubbing his dad's back. "All that was so long ago anyway." He glanced round at the ranch hands who were all looking uncomfortable witnessing this display of emotion from their boss. "Come on guys, drink up," he said. "Annie's gonna get your dinner ready now — aren't you Annie?"

"Right." Annie bustled from the room, signalling that all of them should follow her into the dining room. Parker hung back, putting his hand on Royce's shoulder.

"You all right?"

Royce covered Parker's hand with his own. "Yeah...go on. Dad and I will be through in a minute." He knelt by Aaron's feet and wrapped his arms about him. "Dad, I don't want you feeling bad about any of that. I know I was upset at the time, but I'm not anymore. Mom understood your reasons, too."

Aaron looked up and met his son's eyes through his tears. "You're a good boy, Royce. A lot of kids would've hated me for what I did...but you, you've always been a good boy..."

God, Royce thought. *Would he still be saying that if he knew what I'd been doing with his foreman?* "C'mon, Dad. Let's go join the others. Annie'll be madder than a hornet if you don't eat her cookin'."

Later that night, after the men left and Annie and his dad had gone to bed, Royce and Parker stood out by the corral talking together in low voices.

"Your dad thinks the world of you," Parker said, his hand squeezing Royce's shoulder.

"He was a mite drunk."

"Still, the truth often comes out with the liquor. You sing real purty, by the way."

"Thanks."

"So, you wanted to be in show business?"

Royce sighed. "Yeah…but it didn't happen for reasons that you've probably figured out. That's yesterday's news—and the reason I went to law school. Oh…"

"What?"

"I just remembered, Dad said there was a letter for me. I forgot all about it. Ah, it can wait till tomorrow."

"Maybe important…"

"Maybe…but what's more important is my wanting you to kiss me like you mean it."

"I always mean it."

"Prove it."

"Right here?"

"Well, that moon's kinda bright, so maybe behind the barn."

"Behind the barn? What are we—kids?"

Royce chuckled and took Parker's hand, leading him away from the corral and towards the bunkhouse. "Jim said they were all going into town, so let's take advantage of that. You can yell as loud as you want."

"Sex pig…"

"Oink, oink…"

Their clothes were torn from their bodies even before they made it inside Parker's room. Locked in each other's arms, they careened across the floor before collapsing on Parker's bed. Royce giggled as the bedsprings groaned and clanked under their combined weight.

"Has it ever seen this kind of action before?" he mumbled against Parker's lips.

"Never." Parker's tongue slid into Royce's mouth, effectively stopping all conversation. His hands stroked and caressed the smooth skin on Royce's back, travelling over the round swell of his butt, pulling him into the heat of his crotch, grinding their erections together. Jesus, but this man felt so wonderful in his arms. Every part of him, so vibrant, so vital and so willing to be his.

Never had Parker known feelings like the ones that now coursed through his mind and body, filling him with such elation and happiness. He had truly found the one who could make him feel that what lay ahead for him was to be shared with this beautiful man. How had he gotten so lucky? What had he done to deserve someone as wonderful as Royce?

"Stop thinking, and keep kissing," Royce mumbled. "You think too much, y'know."

"One of us has to," Parker said. He grinned and kissed the tip of Royce's nose.

Royce stretched his taut body over Parker's. "Love you, Cowboy."

"Love you, too. Why don't you bring that thing that's throbbin' between my legs up here so I can show my appreciation?" Royce obeyed, straddling Parker's chest and letting the head of his cock rest on Parker's lips.

"Mmm…" Parker opened wide and took all of Royce into his mouth. Their eyes met as Parker savoured the length of Royce's cock, and through his ecstasy, Royce smiled, his mind and being filled with the wonder of what they meant to one another, and how right it all felt. He held Parker's face between his hands, and slipped out of his mouth, lowering his body over Parker's till their mouths met. Suddenly, to hold Parker and be held and kissed by him meant more to him than anything else in the world.

"I love you," he whispered against Parker's lips. "Stay with me, always."

"You know I will," Parker said, his voice gruff with the emotion Royce's words brought him. "I told you. You're mine, Royce. Forever."

That night, their lovemaking transcended the sexual to join them as one, both physically and spiritually, and as they lay quietly in each other's arms, the giant unasked question in both their minds was — what now?

Chapter Seven

Royce rolled out of his bed and padded into the bathroom. Even from up in his room, the aroma of Annie's morning coffee assailed his nostrils, making him look forward to the day ahead.

Another day with Parker.

The memory of the wonderful night they had spent together caused him to smile at his reflection in the mirror. Sometimes, he still couldn't quite believe just how all this had happened — but he sure was glad it had.

After he'd relieved himself, splashed his face with cold water and pulled on his jeans and a sweatshirt, he went downstairs, eager for breakfast. Passing his father's office, he remembered the letter Aaron had said he'd left on the desk. In bold print on the left hand corner it read 'Bancroft, Leininger & Petrinni, Attorneys-at-Law'. Royce whistled softly between his teeth. So, they'd actually deigned to reply, had they? Taken them long enough.

He ripped the envelope open and read what was nothing less than an offer of employment by one of the most influential law offices in California, if not the entire country.

"Wow," he muttered. Then his eyes widened as he saw what they were offering him per annum. "Wow! Hey, Dad...get a load of this!"

* * * *

Parker wiped the sweat from his forehead with his shirt sleeve. "Man, it's hot," he muttered. Northern California in September could really cook sometimes, making fire hazards a very real threat. Everyone in the area was on alert to watch out for possible problems—not only from natural or accidental causes, but also for those fires set by humanity's dregs... arsonists.

He looked across to the ranch house as Aaron strode towards him, looking grim. Uh oh...problems?

"What's up, Boss?"

Aaron kicked at the dirt under his boot and glared about him for a few moments before answering.

"Boss?"

"That damned stubborn kid of mine," Aaron exclaimed, his face flushed with frustration.

"What did he do now?" Parker asked, grinning.

"He's going to turn down the offer of a lifetime, Parker. Something he's studied for, worked for, for the past six years. Now it's in the palm of his hand, and he's goin' to throw it all away."

Parker frowned. "What offer?"

"A position with the biggest law firm in the state, and a salary that, at his age, is incredible. And he's just going to toss it aside, all because he wants to stay here on the ranch."

"Oh…" Parker couldn't think of a thing to say. Of course he knew the reason why—Royce didn't want to leave him. Parker felt a warm glow suffuse his body at the thought that Royce loved him enough to give up what he had once considered more important than anything else.

"And you know, Parker," Aaron was saying, "I can't bully him into taking this job, even though I think he's one crazy kid for turning it down. Years ago, I refused to let him do what he wanted—I can't do it again. Wrong as I think he is, I'll support his decision."

Parker nodded, then said, "He might change his mind once he's thought it through."

Aaron put his hand on Parker's arm. "I wondered if you would speak to him about it. You and Royce have become good friends over the weeks since your accident. He looks up to you—he's told me that. Maybe he would listen to you…"

"Well…I'll try, but you know Royce. Once he gets an idea about something, it's hard to get him to change his mind." *And I should know*, Parker thought ruefully. Royce could twist him round his little finger with that cute look on his face. Damn it…he didn't want Royce to leave either, but was this the right decision? What his dad had said about studying and working so hard all these years—and now to just throw it aside? *For me*, he thought. *For me.*

"I'd appreciate it, Parker. I just don't want to see the years of sacrifice go to waste."

"Where is he?"

"He went into town. Annie needed some stuff so he said he'd go for her."

"Okay. I'll talk to him when he gets back."

Parker watched Aaron stride off towards the stable, his mind trying to cope with what he knew he should do, but was unwilling to say the words that would make it happen. He knew Royce wouldn't listen to anyone's words, even his, encouraging him to take the job—he'd just laugh and press his body to Parker's, nibble his ear, and say, "Forget it Parker...this is where I want to be...with you."

But he was letting his old man down—the one who wanted to see him succeed on his own terms in life. Yes, the ranch was a viable future, but it wasn't Royce's—not yet. To become a high-powered lawyer in a prestigious company was what he had strived for. That should be his future. *But with me hanging on his neck, it won't happen.* So, drastic measures have to be taken. Measures that are gonna hurt like hell. *Maybe down the line, when Royce has fulfilled his father's dreams, and some of his own, maybe I can tell him the reason I did it...make amends.*

Grimly he pulled his cell phone from his back pocket and punched in Royce's number.

"Hey..." Royce's voice was warm and intimate, and Parker's resolve began to waver. Dammit, he couldn't do this!

"Royce, we need to talk."

"Sure. You sound funny. You okay?"

"Yeah, I'm fine, but can you meet me down by the river in say...an hour?"

"You bet, Cowboy—and I'll come prepared!"

"No. We need to talk is all."

"Oh, okay..." Now Royce sounded puzzled, and Parker hung up before he had to explain further.

"God dammit," he muttered. "How am I goin' to get through this?"

* * * *

Royce's truck was already there when Parker pulled in under the trees. He found him lying on his back by the river, hat off, his hands clasped behind his head, his eyes closed like he was dozing. Parker stood for a moment, silently watching him. *God, but he is beautiful,* he thought. All the way from the ranch, he'd been rehearsing what he was going to say, but now he knew the words were going to stick in his throat.

"I know you're there, Parker," Royce said without turning his head or opening his eyes.

Parker dropped to his knees beside him. "How'd you know?"

"I always know when you're near." He drew Parker in for a kiss, and at the touch of his lips Parker felt himself go weak. His mouth opened to Royce's, his hand slipped inside his shirt, gently teasing Royce's left nipple. Then he pulled away with a suddenness that made Royce gasp with surprise.

"What's wrong?"

"Like I said, we need to talk."

Royce sat up, leaning on one elbow, his eyes gazing into Parker's filled with concern.

"Okay…"

"Royce…I…shit…I just can't do this anymore."

"Do what?"

"I can't be with you anymore."

"*What?*" Royce looked like Parker had just slapped him across the face. Then he blinked, and a half smile crossed his face. "You're joking, aren't you? You're pulling my leg."

"No, Royce, I'm not joking. I mean it. You and me, we're through. I'm sorry, but there it is. You're a great kid and—

"Stop it!" Royce yelled. "Stop it right now, Parker. This is not funny!"

"It's not meant to be funny. I'm dead serious." Parker flinched as he saw the fury build in Royce's expression.

"You son-of-a-bitch!"

The punch to his jaw took Parker by surprise. With a grunt of pain, he fell onto his back, while Royce sprang to his feet, glaring down at him.

"Tell me you're lying, Parker," he yelled.

Parker rolled away from him and stood up, rubbing his jaw. "I'm not lyin' Royce. I just don't want this to go on any longer."

"*This*? You take the love I have for you, all the times together when you said you loved me, all the times you *fucked* me—and call it *this*? What does *this* mean to you, Parker?"

"Royce…I…God dammit, don't make this harder than it is!"

"What? I should just say, oh, okay Parker, we're through—no big deal? You piece of shit, Parker. I love you, and you just expect me to act like nothing's happened? You've broken my heart, Parker. D'you understand that?"

"Yes," Parker mumbled, looking down. "Yes, I understand…"

The next moment he felt Royce's body slam into him, knocking him flat on his back. Royce sat astride him, his tear filled eyes blazing with anger and hurt.

"That's right, Royce, hit me if it'll make you feel better."

"Parker!" Royce brought his clenched fists down hard on Parker's chest. "*Parker*…You said you loved me. Just last night you said that I was yours…no one else's…*yours*—and I believed you, Parker. I believed you!"

A great wrenching cry was torn from him as he fell over onto his side and lay, crumpled up into a tight ball, his hands over his face while he sobbed his heart out.

Jesus Christ. Parker watched with a sense of horror as the man he loved fell apart in front of his eyes. He'd known this was going to be rough. He'd thought Royce would get mad and call him names, but he hadn't expected this. Tentatively, he touched Royce's shoulder.

"Royce…"

"Go away, Parker." Royce's voice was flat and hollow.

"I…I don't want to leave you like this."

Royce lifted his tear-streaked face to Parker's. "Then, just how did you want to leave me? What did you expect my reaction to be? Me, standing all clear-eyed and noble while you slouched away, your hat in your hands? Well, it's not going to be like that, you fucking bastard. Just keep out of my sight 'til I leave the Double R." He pushed himself to his feet and stared at Parker, his eyes as hard as flint. "If I was as cold and unfeeling as you, I'd tell my dad to fire your sorry ass, but don't worry, I won't sink that low." Picking up his hat, he turned his back on Parker and walked quickly away.

It took every ounce of Parker's willpower to stop from running after him and telling him he didn't mean a word of what he'd just said. Instead he sat by the river, tears of loss springing to his eyes. If he lived to be a hundred, he would never forget the look of complete contempt Royce had thrown at him before he walked away. Nor would he ever forgive himself for hurting the only man he had ever truly loved.

Chapter Eight

One year later

"And that was the last time you ever saw him?" Charles Fletcher looked across the table at Royce, his brown eyes filled with sympathy.

Royce nodded. "I haven't been back to the ranch since then. Dad and Annie came down to LA last Christmas. We had a nice time."

"Why d'you suppose he broke off with you so abruptly?"

"Charles, I have asked myself that question a million times over the past year. Just the night before, we had a little party at the house, to celebrate Parker winning the grand prize at the rodeo. My dad got a little tipsy and asked me to sing, and when I was through, I saw tears in Parker's eyes. Afterwards, he and I made love like it was for the very first time – so sweet, so incredibly sweet – and hot. I'll never forget it."

"And I suppose no one you've met here in LA comes close."

"How did you guess?"

"But you've been out on dates…that Carter guy…"

"Carter's a nice guy, but there's no heat between us. I think Parker's screwed me for having feelings for anyone else."

"Oh, give it time, Royce. You're a good looking dude, on your way to being junior partner in California's most prestigious law firm. Someone's gonna snap you up, one of these days."

"What about you, Charles?"

"You're not my type. Too pretty."

Royce chuckled. "Thanks, but I meant, who're you seeing these days?"

"Oh, no one and everyone." Charles winked at him. "I believe there's safety in numbers."

"As long as you're safe."

"Yes, Mother, I'm always safe."

Over the course of Royce's first year in the law firm of Bancroft, Leininger and Petrinni, he and Charles had become fast friends. Charles was short and slender— "*Petit*," he liked to say. "Except where it counts!" Full of energy and gifted with a wicked sense of humour, he'd befriended Royce almost immediately. For all his clever retorts, Charles was insightful and warm-hearted and had seen in Royce, a man who'd been wounded, and whose trust had been sorely tested.

Even so, it had taken Royce this long to fully open up to Charles about his relationship with Parker and the disastrous toll the breakup had taken on his self confidence. The offer of employment with the law firm in LA had been a life saver in a way, throwing him into a hectic but rewarding schedule. Royce had given it everything he had, and his efforts had not gone unnoticed.

What Charles had intimated about his role as junior partner was most definitely on the cards for next year.

"So, you're still in love with this guy?" Charles asked.

Royce rolled his eyes and polished off his vodka martini before answering. "If you're going to think I'm lame by answering 'yes', then the answer's 'no'."

"When in fact the answer's 'yes'," Charles said quietly.

"Yes, I'm afraid that's the answer." Royce tried desperately to stop the tears welling behind his eyes. "You have no idea, Charles, how many times I have called myself a fool for the way I feel—but dammit, I just can't forget him. I'm fine when I'm at work, although even then, sometimes the thought of him will come to me, and I'll just stop whatever I'm doing, and it's like I can feel his presence, smell his scent. But at night, it's pathetic. *I'm* pathetic. I can't tell you how many times I've jerked off just thinking of him. Sorry, too much information, right?"

"No, no…it's okay." Charles shook his head in wonder. "Shit, Royce, I have never felt that way about anyone."

Royce laughed ruefully. "Consider yourself lucky."

"No really…I know this has been rough on you, but don't you sometimes think back on the wonderful times you and he had together? I mean, it sounds like he really loved you too."

"Yeah, I think he did for a while. And you're right, when he did, it was fantastic. Unfortunately, that's what makes it all the harder to forget. You see, I live on those memories."

* * * *

Parker sat in Aaron's truck waiting for him to finish his phone call inside the house. They were driving into town for provisions — something Aaron liked the two of them to do ever since Royce had left for LA. The old man liked the company, he said, and Parker knew he missed his son a lot. Parker missed him, too. More than missed him, he thought now. He'd longed for him every day and night since he'd been gone. He'd never considered it remotely possible that he could miss another human being as much as he did Royce.

Shit, when he and Drew had parted company he'd gotten over it in a matter of days — but this, this aching loneliness that seemed to settle on him like a black cloud of despair every time he thought of how they'd parted — of *why* they'd parted. And now, as he thought of it, had he been totally stupid to have done it that way? What if he had just encouraged Royce to take the position in LA — maybe that would have been enough. They could've visited one another — hell, LA wasn't that far away. An hour on the plane and Royce would have come home for the holidays — Christ but he missed him so much.

"Okay, Parker — sorry to keep you waitin' there." Aaron pulled the truck door open. "Damned banker wants to bend my ear forever." He climbed in behind the wheel and started the engine. "Here." He handed Parker a folded piece of paper. "Annie's been adding to the list the whole time I've been on the phone. I told her she's goin' to bankrupt me one of these days." He glanced at Parker as he pulled out onto the main road. "So, how you doin', son?"

"I'm fine, boss."

"You don't look fine — kinda piqued, if you ask me. You not sleeping?"

"I'm fine," Parker said, again. "Really fine."

"You're a liar, Parker. Just like Royce is a liar."

"'Scuse me?" Parker shot Aaron a look of alarm.

"I ask Royce how he is every time he phones – 'I'm fine Dad,' he says. 'Just fine.' But I can hear it in his voice. He's lonesome."

"But I thought he was doin' really good at that fancy law firm he works for," Parker protested.

"Oh yeah, he's doin' real good. Up for junior partner, he says. They all think the sun shines outta his backside."

"Well then…"

"But it's not what he really wants, Parker." Aaron sighed long and hard. "You know, years ago I hurt my boy, and I have regretted it ever since. Now, I feel like he did this just to please me. He wanted to stay here on the ranch, and I guess I kinda gave him what-for about it, then all of a sudden he changed his mind and went off to LA. I know you said you'd talk to him about it, but…"

Parker listened to Aaron, his eyes fixed on the road ahead. He stiffened in his seat as a hay truck suddenly appeared, as if from nowhere, in front of them.

"Boss, look out!" Parker instinctively reached for the wheel, but Aaron had wrenched it to one side, sending the truck skittering off the road, down the steep embankment on the far side, where it rolled over and over, before coming to a crunching stop, upside down.

Parker felt like every tooth in his head had been shaken loose. He could taste blood as he hung there suspended by his seatbelt.

"Boss, you all right?"

Aaron didn't answer him, and a quick look assured Parker the older man was unconscious. "Shit…" Parker unhooked his seat belt and crawled out of the open window. Smoke poured from the crumpled engine block.

He ran to the driver's side, a bolt of pain shooting through his right leg.

"You all right down there?"

Parker looked up to see the driver of the hay truck peering down at him.

"Yeah, but I'll need a hand getting my boss outta here," he yelled.

With the driver's help Parker managed to ease Aaron's unconscious body out through the window just before a lick of flame erupted from the engine, and almost immediately the truck was enveloped in fire. Between them, they managed to haul Aaron up the embankment and onto the road, where they waited for the ambulance and the police to arrive.

The next three or four hours were like a nightmare for Parker. The ride to the hospital had seemed interminable, and while he had to admit the paramedics appeared to know what they were doing, he couldn't help but fret over the delay in getting Aaron to the hospital. Aaron looked so darned pale and seemed unresponsive, but when he tried asking the paramedics questions, he was told they were doing their best, and he should just sit tight. Once they'd arrived at the hospital, Aaron was admitted to an ICU ward immediately, and Parker had to wait outside, fretting some more. When a doctor finally came out to apprise him of Aaron's condition, Parker asked what was uppermost in his mind. Should he call Mr. Chandler's son, Royce? And the answer had been yes.

Parker stared at the cell phone that lay in the palm of his hand. Jesus…this was going to be the hardest thing he'd ever done in his life—apart from when he'd told Royce all those lies about not loving him anymore. He groaned softly to himself as he punched in the number he'd found in Aaron's billfold along with a photograph of Royce on his graduation day. Staring at Royce's handsome face lit up with the sunny smile he remembered so well had caused his heart to constrict with pain. How was he going to feel when Royce arrived here in person? How was Royce going to feel? What would they possibly say to one another?

He listened to Royce's voice telling him he couldn't take his call but to leave a message. Parker cleared his throat.

"Hey Royce, it's Parker. I'm afraid your dad's had a serious accident. He's in St. Anne's. They've stabilised him for the time being, but the docs think you should come home as soon as you can." He left his number and said goodbye.

* * * *

When Royce got home, he listened to the message in disbelief. Tears sprang to his eyes as he listened to the soft sexy voice on his answering machine—the voice he'd thought he would never hear again and with news he'd never wanted to hear at all.

"Oh, Jesus...*Dad*..." Despite his grief, Royce couldn't talk to Parker about this. Quickly he dialled the house, hoping to speak to Annie first, but as he heard the answering machine pick up, he realised that, of course, she would have already left for hospital. Biting his lip, he punched in Parker's number.

"Hey, Royce..."

Parker's voice sighing in his ear made Royce's breath catch in his throat, but he made his own voice sound cold and differential.

"How is he?"

"They got him stabilised, but he's still in ICU. You comin' up?"

"Of course. Is Annie there?"

"Yeah, she's right here."

"Let me speak to her, please."

"Okay. See you later then."

Royce did not reply but waited as Parker handed his cell phone to Annie. If Parker thought for one minute that this was going to change anything between them, he was sorely mistaken.

After he spoke with Annie, Royce called the airline and reserved a seat on the first available plane to Sacramento.

All the way there, Royce's mind was a jumble of apprehension, anticipation and regrets. As if it wasn't bad enough that his father was lying seriously hurt in intensive care, he was going to have to face the man who had broken his heart. Maybe Parker would have enough class to make himself scarce before he got there, but somehow, Royce doubted that. No, there'd he be, looking suitably hangdog, just waiting for a kind word from him — fat chance!

Jim Ballard, his dad's long-time employee and close friend, was at the airport ready to drive him to the hospital. Thank God. At least Parker had enough sense not to meet him himself.

"Your dad will be glad to see you when he comes to," Jim said, as he steered his truck out of the airport.

"How is he?"

"Still unconscious, but you know your old man, he's as stubborn as a mule. This won't keep him down for long."

"How did it happen?"

"Parker and him were going into town—"

"Parker was driving?" Royce asked sharply.

"No, your dad was at the wheel. Seems like some fool hay truck driver swung out in front of them. Your dad got the worst of the deal. Parker was lucky to just have a twisted knee and a bloody lip."

Royce fell silent. He'd been so ready to blame Parker for the whole thing, and he hadn't even been driving the truck.

"Just as well Parker was there," Jim was saying. "Truck went up in flames after he dragged your dad out of it."

"Oh Jesus," Royce murmured. Now he was going to have to thank Parker for saving his father's life. How was he ever going to stay calm enough to do that?

It was a short run from the airport to St. Anne's, and Royce's heart hammered in his chest as he and Jim hurried through the corridors towards the ICU. He was nervous to see his dad in this state, but he couldn't deny that a great deal of his apprehension was due to the inevitable confrontation he would have with Parker.

"In here, son," Jim said, pushing the door to the ICU open.

Parker was the first person Royce saw when he entered the waiting room. For a long, intense moment, the two men stared at each other across the room, neither one moving or speaking. Then Annie ran forward and flung her arms around Royce.

"Oh, I'm sorry you had to come home to this," she cried, her face on his chest.

Royce kissed the top of her head. "He's going to be all right, Annie. You know my dad. He's too ornery to give up." His eyes met Parker's again over the top of Annie's head. "Parker," he said, nodding slightly. Keeping his arm around Annie, he walked the few steps that separated them. "I want to thank you for saving my father's life. Jim tells me you pulled him from the truck before it burned up."

Parker took a step forward then winced as his knee gave him hell. "I'm just glad I was there."

Royce pretended he hadn't noticed Parker's obvious discomfort. "Well then," he said. "I'll go in and see him. Come with me, Annie?"

Together, he and Annie entered the ICU ward, leaving Parker and Jim outside. Aaron lay still and pale on the hospital bed, the lower part of his face covered by an oxygen mask. His head was bandaged, and his left arm was in a cast. A nurse, standing by the bed monitoring Aaron's vital signs, looked up as they entered.

"You must be Mr. Chandler's son, Royce," she said, smiling.

Royce nodded.

"He's doing quite well, at the moment. I'll let the doctor know you're here, and he can fill you in on all the details."

"How extensive are his injuries?" Royce asked.

"Cuts and bruises mostly, a fractured bone in his left forearm, and the concussion of course—no skull fractures, though. I'll just get the doctor for you."

Still smiling, she left them, closing the door quietly behind her. Royce looked down at his father's pale face and tears welled in his eyes. He took Aaron's hand in his and squeezed it gently.

"Come on, Dad," he whispered. "Please wake up. I'm here to see you get well and I'm not leaving 'til you do. So if you want me to keep my job, you'll wake up and tell me you're okay." He wiped away his tears with the back of his hand. "Come on, Dad…please…"

Annie took his arm to comfort him. "He can hear you, I know," she said. "He's doing his best to come back to us."

"Mr. Chandler?" The doctor's quiet voice behind him made Royce start involuntarily. "Sorry, I didn't mean to startle you." He held out his hand. "I'm Doctor Jessup…"

Royce stared at the older, distinguished looking man and took his proffered hand. "Is he going to be all right?" he asked, abruptly.

Jessup smiled. "We're quite encouraged by his progress so far. When he regains consciousness, we'll have a better idea about his motor functions, but so far, there's no sign of any permanent damage."

Royce breathed a sigh of relief and smiled at Annie who kissed his cheek. "D'you have any idea when he might wake up, Doctor?"

"That's a little harder to predict. There's no real reason why he shouldn't wake up tonight or tomorrow, but sometimes it can take longer. He will require extensive bed-rest and physical therapy once he's released."

Royce nodded. "Well, I'd like to stay with him tonight, if that's all right?"

"Of course. We'll have a cot brought in for you later. Well," he held out his hand again. "I'll see you in the morning on my rounds. If you need anything, just let the nurse know."

"Thanks." Royce shook Jessup's hand. "Annie," he said after the doctor had left. "Why don't you have Jim drive you home? I'll be all right here by myself. I brought a book."

"If you're sure. I am kinda tired."

"Off you go then. If there's any change in his condition, I'll call you right away."

"Okay. Goodnight, darlin'." She gave him another kiss then went to tell Jim and Parker they should all leave.

Royce pulled up a chair and sat by his father's side. For a long time, he just stared at Aaron's face, willing him to wake up and get on with his life. *Lord, he's going to be so pissed when he realises what happened, and how long it's going to take for him to be back on his feet, running the ranch again. Better go bring my bag in from the waiting room*, he thought, getting up from the chair.

He opened the door then started with surprise on seeing a familiar figure seated on one of the chairs in the waiting room.

"You're still here," he remarked as he picked up his bag.

Parker looked at him with a sad expression. "I wondered if you'd feel like talkin'."

"Talking?" Royce gave a snort of derision. "What on earth would we talk about, Parker? Look, I'm really grateful that you saved my father's life, but—"

"Not about that," Parker interrupted, standing up. "About what happened with you and me."

"You *must* be joking," Royce snapped, raising his voice. "There is nothing you could say about that subject that would interest me." He turned away and stepped inside the ICU ward. "Go away, Parker. You don't belong here."

"Like hell I don't!"

Royce stumbled back into the room as Parker barged in. "What the hell?"

"I belong here, Royce," Parker said, his face tinged with anger. "Don't you ever say otherwise. That man there, he means everything to me. He's been like a father to me, so don't say I don't belong!"

"Keep your damn voice down, Parker," Royce seethed. "You have some fucking nerve after what you did."

"What I did," Parker said, lowering his voice, "was make sure you got what you'd strived for all those years of studyin' and workin' hard for your future. Your daddy told me you were ready to throw it all away, to stay on the ranch — and I knew why."

"Of course, you knew why. You were the fucking reason, Parker, and you threw it all in my face."

"I was lyin' —"

"Damned straight you were lying — you're the biggest liar I've ever had the misfortune to meet! Telling me you loved me, Parker. Making me believe it, and all the while just laughing up your sleeve at the boss's poor, gullible, asshole son. Christ, when I think about it, I could fucking kill you!"

"I wasn't lyin' about that, Royce."

"Oh, please —"

"I love you, Royce."

Royce stared at him long and hard, then his mouth twisted with contempt. "Get out of here, Parker, before I forget where we are."

"Just listen to me for one minute! I wasn't lying to you about loving you — I lied when I said I didn't love you." Parker's shoulders slumped with despair as he continued. "I had some cockamamie idea that if I did that, you'd up and leave and go to LA. That you'd be doing what your daddy wanted for you, without me getting in the way. After you left, I cursed myself for a fool a million and one times, but, when I heard you were doin' so well, I just couldn't find the way to let you know that I missed you like I've never missed anyone before in my whole stupid life. And tonight, seeing you again, even under these circumstances...it was like everything I ever wanted."

"Oh, Parker..." Royce could not believe what he was hearing. "You stupid asshole. You dumb, stupid, *wonderful* jerk! I could kill you..."

94

"Well…" Parker gave him a lopsided grin. "Maybe, just a flesh wound?"

Royce stumbled into Parker's arms, their lips meeting in a scorching kiss, but anything that might have followed was curtailed as Aaron let out a long, deep groan from under his oxygen mask.

"Dad!" Royce bounded to his side. "Dad, can you hear me?"

Aaron mumbled something neither of them could understand.

"I'll get the nurse," Parker yelled, running from the room.

Carefully, Royce lifted the oxygen mask from his father's face. "Dad," he whispered. "Are you all right?"

His father's eyes met his. "I shouldn't be," he said, his voice weak but audible. "After what I just heard."

Royce blanched. "Oh, Dad…you heard what Parker and I were talking about?"

"How the hell could I not hear? The pair of you were yellin' loud enough for everyone in the county to hear."

"Oh, Dad…"

"We'll talk about this later, Royce — the three of us — once I'm outta here."

Just then, Parker and the nurse burst into the room.

"Oh, Mr. Chandler," the nurse gushed. "What a wonderful recovery! It must have been your son's presence that brought you back to us."

"You could say that," Aaron growled. "I need to pee!"

Watching the nurse fuss over his father, Royce pulled Parker outside into the waiting room. "He heard everything," he said, his eyes on Parker's.

"Whoa…you mean, *everything*?"

"Everything."

"Oh, shee-it!"

"Right...shee-it, Parker. What are you going to do about it?"

"What am I going to do about it?"

Royce grinned at him. "Well, let's see...you could say you were lying again. Of course, he'll never believe you."

Parker groaned, then looking around quickly to make sure they were alone, he grabbed Royce and kissed him hard on the lips. "One thing I'm not gonna do this time around—"

"Yeah?" Royce nibbled on Parker's bottom lip. "What's that?"

"Let you outta my sight again!"

"You boys better get in here!" They sprang apart as the nurse called out. "Mr. Chandler has something to say to you."

Royce and Parker exchanged looks of apprehension. Oh God, Royce thought, as they entered the ICU room together. What if he *fired* Parker? It would kill his cowboy...and him...

Aaron gave the nurse a little smile. "Would you mind letting me talk to my men in private? There's some stuff you'd find pretty boring—you know, business."

"Oh, of course," she twittered, picking up her clipboard and heading for the door. "I'll just call the doctor and tell him the good news."

Aaron stared at Royce and Parker for a long moment without saying anything.

"Dad..." Royce moved to his side. "Parker and I—"

"I know all about you and Parker...now," his father said, his expression difficult for either man to read. "You have to admit that coming to in a hospital room and listening to your son and your foreman acting like a couple of lovesick teenagers just might be a tad traumatic."

"Oh, Dad…"

"Royce." Aaron glared up at his son. "If you say 'Oh, Dad' one more time in that pathetic way, big as y'are, I will tan your hide!"

Parker let out an involuntary snort of laughter, then promptly wished he hadn't as Aaron glared at him.

"And you, Parker. I thought I knew you, but you're just as big an idiot as my son!" Aaron struggled to sit up. "Well, come on. Don't stand there gawking at me like the idiots y'are. Give me a hand, God dammit!"

"Dad, take it easy," Royce protested, slipping his arm under his father's and easing him up on the pillow. "The doctor's going to be mad as hell if you overdo things right away."

"And what do you call what you two were doing earlier? That wasn't overdoing it? All that angst flying around in here."

"Boss…" Parker shuffled his feet in discomfort. "Royce and me…well, he wasn't the one who started this."

"Oh hush up, Parker," Aaron growled. "I know my boy well enough to know he has a will of his own. If you're tryin' to tell me you seduced him, I'll know you're lyin'." Aaron closed his eyes for a moment before continuing. "Look," he said finally, "this isn't something I saw coming. I knew you two were close. Annie and I talked about it, wondering why since Royce left, you both seemed to have drifted apart. Well, now I know the reason, and while I can't say I'm over the damned moon about it, if my son has to spend the rest of his life with another fella, then I guess I'm glad it's you, Parker."

"Oh, Dad…"

"There you go again, with your 'Oh, Dad' bullshit. Now cut it out—and get outta here, the pair of you. I don't need you here hovering over me all night—and you both need to talk about a lot of stuff. Go find yourselves a hotel—"

"Dad!"

"Royce!"

The three men stared at one another for a few seconds before bursting out with laughter.

Royce sat on the bed and hugged Aaron. "You are the best father in the whole world," he said, kissing his cheek. "Can I come home now?"

"It's up to you, son."

"Thanks, Dad." He looked up at Parker. "Will you take me on, foreman?"

Parker grinned at him. "I guess I'll give it some thought."

Chapter Nine

The Times Motel wasn't exactly the best establishment in Sacramento, but it was only a block from St. Anne's Hospital, and neither Royce nor Parker could stand to waste anymore time looking around for a more romantic hideaway.

"I don't care where we go," Royce said, his hand inside Parker's shirt, his fingers teasing Parker's right nipple. "Just make it quick!"

"How 'bout right here in the truck?"

"That'll work."

"No, wait..." Parker brought Royce's hand to his lips. "We need room to stretch out. I want to feel every inch of your bare skin on mine."

"Okay, you got me. Let's check in."

As soon as they entered the room, Royce headed for the shower. "C'mon you," he said, grabbing Parker's hand. "It's been a long day. I need a shower, and I don't want you out of my sight for a moment."

"I was goin' to order champagne from room service," Parker said, straight-faced.

Royce chuckled, then held Parker close. "I have some Scotch in my bag. I figured I was going to need a drink after seeing you again. I didn't think for one moment I'd need it for a celebration."

Their kiss was long and sweet with an undercurrent of passion and longing. Feeling the warmth and strength of Parker's arms about him, Royce could scarcely believe that this was happening. The man he loved and had thought lost to him forever was holding him, kissing him, bringing him all the wonderful sensations he'd tried to keep alive in his mind for over a year.

"Parker, Parker," he murmured. "I love you, I love you."

"Love you, too." Parker tightened his arms around Royce, unwilling to let him go for even a second. "Fuck the shower," he growled, pulling at Royce's shirt. "Just lose your clothes so I can see what I've been missing for over a year." They fell across the bed, locked in each other's arms, the kiss they shared going on and on. They couldn't get enough of one another — their hands, mouths, lips and tongues finding each and every part of each other's bodies. Clothes and boots were ripped off and thrown aside as a frantic need for fulfilment overtook them.

Royce kissed and licked his way over Parker's torso, going slow, savouring the taste, the smell and the feel of the body he could never forget. Parker's body was even harder than he remembered, the muscles even more tightly defined, the ridges of his abdomen etched in sharp relief on the smooth planes of his torso. Royce's lips caressed the head of Parker's cock, his tongue flicking at the slit, lapping up the pre-cum that leaked from it. He felt dizzied by the familiar salty-sweet taste. He writhed in ecstasy as he felt his own cock being taken into the heat of Parker's mouth.

Parker ran his tongue around the velvet skin of Royce's cock head, loving the feel and the taste of his lover's hard flesh. His lips slid down the length, as Royce thrust slowly into his mouth. Parker heard Royce whimper, and he'd have smiled if his mouth hadn't been so full of cock. He grasped Royce's butt, massaging the cheeks, pushing his middle finger all the way into the tight puckered hole. Royce lifted his hips to meet the pressure of Parker's finger, wriggling his butt to help it on its way. Parker shifted, releasing Royce's cock, and knelt behind him. He winced as his bad knee reminded him of what had happened earlier in the day.

"What's wrong?" Royce asked with concern

"Darned knee."

Royce chuckled. "Sorry…but that reminded me of our first time—with your back."

"Ain't gonna stop me from fucking you," Parker growled, placing his hands on Royce's hips and pulling him against his hard cock.

"That's the good news." Royce chuckled again. He reached inside the side pocket of his bag and pulled out a condom packet. He flipped it over his shoulder, and it landed on the small of his back. "Go for it, Cowboy. Ride me hard!"

Parker grabbed the condom and ripped the packet open. "Man, you haven't changed one bit," he said, concentrating on rolling the rubber over his engorged cock. "You're still the sex pig I knew."

"Lucky you." Royce turned to give him a grin. His eyes widened. "Whoa. Did that dick of yours get even bigger?"

"Dunno. You'll be the judge of that." Parker lubed up his fingers with saliva and inserted one, then two, into Royce's anus. "Yeah," he sighed as Royce groaned under him.

"Fuck me, Parker. Fill me up like you used to. I need you, Parker...love you so much."

Parker leaned forward, his cock pushing past Royce's brief resistance with a deep thrust.

"Oh...yes..." Royce pushed up into Parker's crotch, taking every inch of his throbbing manhood inside him. He bit his lower lip to ease the burning sensation. It had been over a year since he'd last felt Parker inside him—a year devoid of sex, filled only with a deep desire to have Parker back in his life and in his arms. Now, his wish had come true, and this beautiful man was once more joined to him, flesh to flesh, soul to soul, and his joy was complete.

Parker gazed down at Royce's smooth, sleek back, at the muscles rippling under his skin as he moved in rhythm with him. He felt like shouting his happiness at the top of his voice—and at the same time bawling like a baby. He'd never imagined that this could happen again—to have Royce here, making love to him as he'd done so many times in his dreams and fantasies. He laid his face on Royce's back and held him tight in his arms, suddenly afraid that this was only a dream, and when he awoke Royce would be gone again.

Royce sensed the subtle shift in Parker's emotions. Carefully, without breaking their union, he eased himself over onto his back, so that he could look up into his lover's face. He reached out and touched Parker's cheek with a tenderness that said it all.

"Love you, Parker," he whispered. "Always did, always will." He wound his legs around Parker's hips, his arms around Parker's torso, holding him close, and at the same time, pulling him even deeper inside himself. Parker pressed their bodies together, kissing him like he'd never been kissed before — never.

"Royce, dammit." Parker murmured, between kisses. "I just can't believe you're here with me again. I've missed you so much, I thought I was goin' crazy sometimes. Every time I thought of the stupid asshole thing I'd done, tellin' you I didn't love you anymore, I could've kicked my own ass. And if it hadn't been for your daddy's accident today, I might never have had the chance to tell you the reason why I lied to you…" He broke off, and held Royce even tighter in his arms.

"Hush, Parker." Royce brushed his lips gently over Parker's. "That's over with. I'm here and you're here, together, where we belong." He bore down on the hard flesh Parker drove into him with a fervour born of passion and desire. All their pent up emotions, their desolation from being so long apart now morphed into the exhilarating joy of being joined as one again. Royce's head fell back as his ecstasy overwhelmed him, and Parker's lips laved the arch of his throat. Their rhythm intensified as their need for each other's fulfilment grew. Their breath came in great panting heaves. Their bodies, slick with sweat, pressed so tight together, it seemed nothing could ever pull them apart.

"*Parker…*" Royce moaned as his orgasm sprang from him in great spurting spasms. He shuddered in Parker's arms, his hands clutching at his lover's flesh as his body bucked in the throes of his ecstasy. Parker kissed him long and hard, gasping into his mouth as his own climax ripped through him like so many electric jolts. It seemed like he would never stop coming.

Together, they collapsed back onto the mattress, arms and legs entwined, their mouths joined in a kiss that went on and on...

* * * *

"You know, I was thinkin', Royce..." Parker gently stroked Royce's chest as he spoke. "I know you asked your daddy if you could come back home—and of course, no one would be happier than me if you did—but is it the right decision for you to make?"

Royce frowned. "What d'you mean?"

"Well, I can't help thinkin' that your talents would be wasted on the ranch when they could be put to more good use in what you're doin'."

"You don't want me to come home?"

Parker kissed him tenderly. "You know I want that more 'n anything, but what if you opened up your own law firm in Sacramento?"

Royce chuckled. "I'm afraid I'm not quite ready for that, Parker. I've only got a year's experience under my belt."

"So what d'you need? Another year or two?"

"At least..."

"Then, why don't you consider it anyway? LA's not so far away. I could fly down to see you, and you could come here for weekends. Would it be so bad?"

"I'd hate being apart from you again."

"But it wouldn't be forever, Royce. We could talk on the phone every day."

"And spend a fortune in airfares."

"It'd be worth it. Your daddy would be so proud. And when you're ready to start your own business, maybe a couple of the fellas from your office would like to join you as partners."

Royce was quiet for a little time, thinking through what Parker had said, then he laughed lightly. "Charles would love it up here in cowboy country."

"Who's Charles?"

"My best buddy in LA. The one I tell all my troubles to."

Parker winced. "Then he knows what a jerk I am."

"He knows I never stopped loving you, Parker. He'll be really happy to hear my good news when I get back."

"Tell him I was just misguided, or somethin'."

Royce turned on his side and kissed Parker sweetly on the lips. Their bodies stretched and arched together in their quiet ecstasy and their joy of being together once again. Royce thrilled to the sensation of Parker's hard, warm body pressed to his.

"If I do go back to LA for a year or two, will you wait for me?"

"You know I will—and like I said, it's not that far away." Parker kissed him again. "You'll do it then?"

Royce nodded. "Mmhmm…if you promise me kisses like that every time we're together."

"I can do even better than that."

"Parker…"

"Yeah?"

"All the time we were apart, I never…uh…did it with anyone else. Did you?"

"Nope…never saw anyone that could take your place." His arms tightened around Royce. "I love you," he murmured, close to Royce's ear. "And I am so glad you're back in my life—this time to stay."

"Forever," Royce whispered, his lips fluttering on Parker's. "I'm yours…forever."

"Darned right y'are," Parker growled. "Even if your daddy says different."

"He won't. The one thing I saw most clearly in his eyes tonight, was that he wanted me to be happy."

"Makes two of us." Parker gave him a slow smile. "Now, what d'you say I start makin' good on that?"

Royce snuggled into his arms. "You've already made me happy, Parker." Then he grinned, and winked. "'Course, I wouldn't mind if you tried for *happier*!"

RIDE 'EM
AGAIN COWBOY

Dedication

For Carol Lynne—thank you for letting me refer to your creation, Cattle Valley, in this story; for Michele Paulin—I'm gonna miss your editing skill and guidance, and of course for my man Phil—always.

Chapter One

Aaron Chandler looked up from the papers he'd been studying as his foreman, Parker Jones, entered the office, a dreamy smile on his face

"Mornin' Boss."

Aaron gave him a knowing look. "You're mighty chipper this morning, Parker. Been talking to Royce, have you?"

"Uh, yes…he called first thing this morning. He'll be here tomorrow noon."

"I know. And you'll most likely talk to him another half dozen times before then. You boys must be rackin' up quite a phone bill between you."

"Well…we got this special rate, y'see…"

Aaron chuckled. "I was just joshin' you, Parker. You found me another hand yet?"

Parker relaxed a little as he prepared to answer. He was always a little uncomfortable when Royce's dad got personal about his relationship with his son. No matter that Aaron had been a captive witness to the two of them reunited after a misunderstanding that had parted them for over a year. Parker had broken up with Royce thinking it was the only way to get him to take the lucrative offer from the law firm where he now worked. Royce had stormed out of Parker's life but had rushed home when Parker called him to let him know his father had been injured in a road accident. While Aaron lay seemingly unconscious in a hospital bed, Royce, on hearing Parker's reason for breaking up with him fell into his arms, and within earshot of his father, declared his undying love for his cowboy.

Aaron had chastised them for making fools of themselves in front of him but had given them his reluctant blessing, saying, "I can't say I'm over the damned moon about it, but if my son has to spend the rest of his life with another fella, then I guess I'm glad it's you, Parker."

"Well?" Aaron looked at him expectantly.

"Oh, yeah—" Parker focused on his boss. "That's why I'm here," he said. "I interviewed this guy from Cattle Valley, Wyoming, yesterday. Name's Miller, Jed Miller. Good references, been a ranch hand for the past five years, assistant foreman for two."

"Why'd he leave Cattle Valley?"

"Personal reasons he says. I didn't aim to pry too much. His references are good…"

"So you said, but personal reasons, Parker? What do you suppose that means?" Aaron frowned and stroked his jaw. "Was he rubbin' someone the wrong way, gettin' into fights? You call up there and talk to anyone?"

"No, I didn't."

"Well, maybe you should."

Parker shuffled his feet. "Boss, I…"

"I know, you don't aim to pry, but I want to know what a fella's about before I hire him. Supposin' he's a trouble maker?"

"Doesn't seem the type to me. Told me right away he was gay. Said he hoped that wasn't a problem. 'Course, him comin' from Cattle Valley I had that figured. So, I told him no problem, and I also told him 'bout Royce and me. Hope you don't mind, Boss."

"I don't mind if you don't, Parker."

"And besides, his references—"

"Yeah, yeah. Well, you haven't let me down yet with your hiring. Bring him in so I can give him a once over."

Parker glanced at his watch. "He should be here in a couple of minutes."

"Good." Aaron waved at the chair by his desk. "Take a load off 'til he gets here. Want some coffee? Annie's brewin' some fresh as we speak."

"Sounds good." He sat in the proffered chair and stretched out his legs.

"So you're lookin' forward to Royce being here, I bet. You met this friend he's bringing?"

"Yeah, Charles. He's quite a character."

Aaron raised an eyebrow. "By that, do you mean he's, uh, *flamboyant*?"

"Not really—well, let me put it this way. He has one helluva sense of humour, can take a joke with the best of 'em—and about his bein' gay, he doesn't hold anything back."

"Hope he doesn't scare some of the boys," Aaron chuckled.

"Oh, they'll be cool with it. They know all about Royce and me."

"But you don't, you know, *swish*."

Parker managed a laugh. "Charles doesn't swish, Boss. He's just a little different. It'll be fine, really. You'll like him."

"Like who?" Annie, Aaron's housekeeper for the past thirty years asked as she bustled in carrying a coffeepot. "Mornin' Parker."

"Mornin' Annie. Uh, Royce's lawyer friend, Charles."

"Oh, yeah!" Annie beamed at Aaron. "I've spoken to him on the phone. Sounds like a really nice fella. *Very* polite."

Parker hid a smile as he thought of all the lurid jokes Charles was famous for.

"What the heck were you yammerin' on the phone to him about?" Aaron asked, looking put out.

"Royce put him on the phone when he called to ask me to make up the spare bedroom," Annie replied tartly. "We had a very nice talk. You'll like him."

"Sounds like I don't have a choice with everyone telling me 'you'll like him'."

A knock at the door had Parker jumping to his feet to answer it. "Hey, Jed—" He grinned at the tall cowboy who reached to shake his hand. "Come on in. Boss, this is Jed Miller, Jed—uh, Mr. Chandler."

"Pleased to meet you, son," Aaron said amicably, taking Jed's hand, approving of the firm shake and calloused fingers. "Come sit, and we'll talk a while."

"Can I get you some coffee?" Annie asked, all smiles.

"That'd be swell," Jed replied, his voice warm and deep.

"I'll just go get another cup."

Parker grinned as Annie flirted with the good looking cowboy. Old enough to be his mother and with three sons of her own, she could still appreciate a fine looking man like Jed. And he was indeed fine looking, Parker thought, admiringly. A shock of copper coloured hair that curled round his ears framed a face that managed to be rugged and gentle at the same time. He wondered what Royce would make of Jed when they met. As usual, thoughts of Royce, and the fact he'd soon be kissing him, and more, gave Parker the start of a hard-on.

He shifted in his seat, clearing his throat at the same time. "Uh, right Jed. Maybe you could give Mr. Chandler a run-down on what your duties were at the Williams' ranch."

"Sure. I was the assistant foreman. Had to take over for Bill Owens, the foreman, when he got sick last fall. I think I did pretty well—no complaints, anyhow."

"So you know what's expected of you," Aaron said.

"Pretty much. 'Course I don't expect your spread to be run exactly like Joe Williams' place. Every boss likes things done their way, and I'm easy with that."

Aaron eyed Jed carefully as he asked, "What kind of personal reasons did you have for leaving Cattle Valley?"

Jed blinked once then his hazel eyes met Aaron's steady gaze straight on. "Will it go against me, if I tell you I'd rather not answer that question?"

"I'd just like to know what kind of man I'd be hiring if I took you on," Aaron said quietly. "I respect your right to privacy, but answer me this. Did it involve stealing or fighting?"

Jed flinched slightly. "No, sir. Definitely not stealing. I've never stolen from anyone, and I'm not likely to in the future. Fighting?" He chuckled softly. "I've been in a couple of fights, but that didn't have anything to do with why I left Cattle Valley. Let's just say it was better I left than hang around. I have no ill feelings towards anyone there, but most likely some people breathed a sigh of relief when I did go."

"That's honest enough." Aaron looked over at Parker. "Well, what do you think, Parker?"

"Joe Williams gave Jed here a good reference," Parker said. "He wouldn't have done that if he didn't think Jed deserved it. I think every man has a right to keep some things to himself, so long as it doesn't have any bearing on his work. I say, hire him."

Jed nodded his thanks at Parker then turned his eyes on Aaron waiting for his decision.

"Well, Jed, Parker hasn't let me down yet," Aaron said. He stood and extended his hand to Jed. "Welcome to the Double R, son. Parker will show you where you can bunk, and introduce you around to the other boys."

Jed grasped Aaron's hand in a strong grip. "Thank you, Mr Chandler. You won't regret your decision to take me on."

Parker caught Aaron's glance and knew his boss was hoping that the tall cowboy's words held more than just the ring of sincerity.

"Come on," he said. "I'll show you where you'll bunk." Parker ushered Jed out of the office. "You bring your stuff with you?"

"Uh, yeah. Back of my Jeep."

"Good. I'll give you a hand taking it over."

"Not much there." Jed heaved a sigh. "Pretty pathetic that at my age I'm still able to carry everything I own in the back of a Jeep."

"Nothin' wrong with that," Parker said. "Belongings just tie a man down."

Jed opened the back of the vehicle and waved at the of boxes and a suitcase. "Not much there to tie me down, I'd say." He glanced at Parker as he hauled the boxes out of the Jeep. "You and Royce — you must be thinking of settling down in your own place one of these days."

"One of these days is right." Parker took the suitcase, and they set off towards the bunkhouse. "He's still got some time to go before he can think of coming up this way. He wants to open his own law firm in Sacramento, so when that happens, I guess we'll be livin' together."

"How do you feel about that?"

Parker shrugged. "Won't know 'til we try it. We get along real good when we're together, here or in Los Angeles, so I don't think it'll be a problem. Here we go…" He pushed open the bunkhouse door and stepped into the large room that served as a kitchen and a place for the men to eat.

"Your room's down there to the right, next to mine." Parker led the way then let Jed pass him into the room that was to be his home for the foreseeable future.

"Nice," Jed murmured, looking around at the small but bright and tidy space. He placed the boxes alongside the nightstand.

"You can thank Royce for the way it looks," Parker told him, handing Jed his suitcase. "He corralled me and a couple of the men into repainting all the rooms then he and Annie went out and got all new curtains, rugs and stuff."

"Looks more like a fancy hotel room than a bunkhouse. What's your room like?"

Parker chuckled. "Even fancier. Royce keeps bringin' me stuff nearly every time he visits." He patted Jed's shoulder and turned to go. "Well, I'll let you get your belongings stowed. Come out to the corral when you're ready, and I'll introduce you around. You'll find them a friendly enough bunch."

"Thanks Parker. See you in a few."

Jed undid the leather straps on his suitcase and flipped open the top. For a long moment, he stood staring down at the case's contents, unable to tear his eyes from the shirt lying on top. Brett's shirt. The shirt he'd left in Jed's room the last time they'd been together—the night they'd had wild, wanton sex that had driven Jed crazy, that he'd never been able to forget. Now, even six months later, as he held the shirt to his face, the sounds and scents of their lovemaking still haunted him, along with the stomach churning words Brett had spoken only a few days later.

"Sorry Jed, shouldn't have happened, you and me... There's someone else in my life."

"Someone else?" Jed had stared at Brett slack-jawed. "But what about all the nights we've spent together, for months now? You never mentioned there was someone else—not once."

"I thought it was all over between us." Brett had the good grace to look shame-faced. "Alan and me, well...he wanted to go live in San Francisco. I didn't and we argued about it, a lot. He finally gave me an ultimatum. Either I went with him or he went alone. I guess my stubborn streak kicked in, and I told him he was goin' alone. That's when I came to work at the Williams' ranch. I didn't hear from him for more than a year then last month..."

And Jed recalled the sudden trip Brett had made 'to visit a sick relative'. Jed hadn't been at all suspicious of the story his tall, sexy lover had spun him. He'd kissed him on his luscious mouth and told him, "Hurry back." Turned out his 'sick relative' was Alan Bennett, a spoiled rotten twink that couldn't make it in San Francisco without Brett and wanted to join him in Cattle Valley.

Jed had told himself he'd be all right. That seeing Alan and Brett together wouldn't bother him. That the smirk Alan wore every time he looked Jed's way wouldn't make him want to smash the supercilious little twit into the ground. But as time went by, he knew the tension that had been created at Joe's ranch was getting to the men. Some thought Brett and Alan should leave and find work elsewhere, but in the end, Jed decided he'd had enough. It was just too damned awkward with the three of them sharing the same bunkhouse, the same table at mealtimes. It got so Jed couldn't stand eating with them. He'd lost weight, his jeans hanging loose on his already rangy frame. But worst of all were the looks of sympathy, and sometimes pity, the other men had cast his way.

His decision to leave had come as no surprise to anyone, even though Joe Williams, the ranch owner, had pretended to be upset when Jed had announced his intention and given a week's notice.

He didn't ask me to reconsider, Jed remembered with some bitterness. Sighing, he picked up the shirt and threw it into the bottom drawer of the pine chest. *Don't know why I kept the darned thing.* Quickly, he unpacked and stowed his clothes in the drawers and small closet then straightening his shoulders, he strode out of his room, heading for the corral where Parker had said he'd wait for him.

Forget what you couldn't have, he told himself, as he had done a hundred or more times before. How'd that song go? "It's a new dawn, it's a new life—" He just wished he was feelin' good.

Chapter Two

Royce guided his friend Charles Fletcher towards the airport exit. As always his heart pounded with excitement at the thought of seeing Parker again and spending the weekend doing all kinds of x-rated things to each other.

"Will you slow down?" Charles panted, twisting his shoulder away from Royce's grip. "Not everyone has legs that go all the way up to our chins, you know? And we're not all about to get bonked by a handsome cowpoke — or should that be poked by a —"

"All right, all right," Royce chuckled, slowing his speedy gait to accommodate his friend's shorter legs. "Sorry, but you know how I get whenever Parker's around."

"Don't I ever. It's embarrassing to be seen out and about with the pair of you. All that kissing and canoodling. You'd think you'd only been together two weeks, not two years."

"We had a year to make up for, don't forget."

Charles sighed. "Oh yes, the year of despondency. Well, you certainly have made up for it, in more ways than one." He nudged Royce's arm. "There's the man of the hour, looking like every gay guy's wet dream come true." He looked over to where Parker stood waiting for them by the exit. His hat was pushed back to reveal his curly black hair, and his shirt was open just enough to give a tantalising glimpse of dark chest hair.

"Can't say I blame you for getting all horny, honey." Charles chuckled as Royce took off like a filly at the starting post, leaving him to plod his way over to where the lovers were already holding each other in a bone-crushing embrace. "What will the neighbours say?" he remarked as Parker let Royce go long enough to notice him standing there.

"Hey, Charlie!" Parker hugged the smaller man to his chest.

"It's Charles, you big galoot," Charles said, laughing. He planted a kiss on Parker's cheek. "I just love how quickly I've taken to the cowboy vernacular around you."

"Yeah, well, don't go callin' the boys at the Double R 'galoots', *Charles*, or you might just get your ass branded."

"Oh, be still my throbbing heart. Let me know who has the longest branding iron, *please*."

Parker rolled his eyes at Royce. "You sure your daddy's ready for the likes of Charles?"

Royce laughed. "He's promised to be as low-key as he can around Dad. You'll see. Dad will like him, just fine."

"That's what Annie and me said earlier, but now I'm not so sure."

"Hey!" Charles punched Parker on the arm. "I'm still here, you know?"

"Like we could forget." Parker threw an arm around both men's shoulders. "Come on then. You guys hungry? I thought we'd stop on the way to the ranch and grab a sandwich or somethin'."

"Sounds good." Royce slipped his arm round his lover's waist and hugged him close. "I've been looking forward to this all week."

"Me too." Parker steered them through the exit door and across to the parking lot. "Hey, Charles, we got us a new hand you might like to say hello to."

"If he looks like you," Charles teased, "I'll give him a very special hello."

"And what might that be?"

Charles laughed. "I don't think Royce will ever let you find out."

"You got that right," Royce growled. "I've heard it said no man is the same after that 'hello'."

"I think Jed could survive it," Parker drawled. "He doesn't strike me as a man who'd go down easy."

"Pun intended?" Charles asked archly.

Parker chuckled. "You know what I mean."

"Sounds like a challenge, Charles," Royce said, winking at his friend. "I'll be interested to watch your progress over the next couple of days."

"You mean someone other than Parker is going to have your attention this weekend?"

"If you make it interesting enough."

The friends laughed together then climbed inside Parker's Jeep and headed into the city.

* * * *

Jed felt pretty good after his first day at the Double R and meeting the men he'd be working with for the foreseeable future. There had been little or no awkwardness expressed by most of the men, and Jed was sure Parker had apprised them of the fact he'd been working in Cattle Valley, the part of Wyoming that was famous, or notorious, depending on a person's views, for its large gay population. Back in his room, he stripped off his shirt then went about unpacking the two boxes that contained what he'd bothered to take with him the day he'd left Cattle Valley for good. The big box contained his saddle and tackle. Couldn't leave that behind—would cost an arm and a leg to replace. The smaller box held a portable compact disc player, a dozen or so discs of his favourite music, a few books, and a photograph album stuffed with photos he'd never bothered to mount properly on the pages—he'd get around to that one of these days, he promised himself.

His fingers stilled over the contents at the bottom of the box. *Shit—the programme for the rodeo Brett and me went to together. Why'd I bring that along?* He pulled the programme from the box and flicked through the colourful pages, the images of cowboys, broncos and roped steers bringing a flood of memories of that perfect day they'd spent alone together and the fantastic sex they'd enjoyed later in their hotel room—fantastic for him anyway. Now, he wondered how good had it been for Brett. Not good enough, obviously, for he'd gone running after that twit Alan soon as he'd whined.

Jed threw himself down on the bed. He closed his eyes and let his mind settle on Brett and the last time they'd made love. He knew he'd never forget it. For him, it had been beautiful, two bodies so perfectly in tune with one another, sweet and hungry kisses that had raised Jed to a level of desire he'd never imagined he could reach. No other man had done it for him before, and he figured, with a quiet desolation, that no man would ever come close again. He groaned as heat gathered in his groin. Just the thought of Brett made him hard. Through the tough denim he stroked the bulge at his crotch, then slowly, almost as though he were teasing himself, he unbuttoned his fly, releasing his hard cock from its confinement. It sprang into his hand, hot and eager for release, the head already glistening with the sticky residue of his pre-cum.

He sank heavily into the mattress as he pumped his hard shaft, running his thumb over the swollen head, using the copious juice that spilled from it as lubricant. A vision of Brett's handsome face and lean body swam before his eyes, and he gave himself up to the memory of the taste and scent of the man. He could almost feel Brett's hands on him, his lips brushing Jed's in the tantalising way he'd had that would drive Jed mad with desire, craving more of that sweet mouth. He shuddered under the weight of the fantasy, now imagining Brett's lips travelling over his fevered skin, Brett's tongue skimming the length of Jed's erection, licking up and down the hot hard flesh before taking it all into the depths of his throat.

His fantasy shifted to the first time he'd fucked Brett—that first fumbling moment when Brett had chuckled softly as Jed struggled to get the condom over his swollen cock.

"Have to get you the extra-large," Brett had kidded, eyeing Jed's thick shaft with admiration. Their moment of levity had done nothing to dampen their ardour, and now Jed groaned softly remembering the sweet warmth that had enveloped him as he'd slid inside Brett's tight eager hole. Brett had felt good, both inside and out, his lithe torso writhing under Jed's hands that stroked and caressed the tight muscles overlain with smooth tanned skin.

"*Ahh...*" A strangled cry erupted from Jed although he'd tried hard to control any noises that could be heard in the neighbouring rooms. His hips bucked as his orgasm rolled over him. Hot cum filled his hand and spattered over his stomach. When his ragged breathing steadied, and his body calmed, the ecstasy that had momentarily been his was replaced by a bitter emptiness and the knowledge that until he got over this obsession with a man he could never have, this was all he'd be left with.

* * * *

Later, after he'd showered and changed into clean clothes, Jed went in search of Parker who'd said he'd be back around three o'clock after picking up Royce at the airport. He really wanted to sit down with Parker and go over what was expected of him on a daily basis. He appreciated the fact that Parker had given him the day before to settle in, but he wouldn't really feel a part of the Double R until he was working. As he approached the ranch house, he saw Parker and two men getting out of Parker's Jeep. One was obviously Royce—easy to know him from the description Parker had given him. Blond, slim and gorgeous—and he was all of that. The other guy was shorter, about five nine at the most, a good, tight build, dark brown hair, and when he bent over to pick up his bag, displayed a nice bubble butt.

Parker, seeing Jed, waved him over. "Hey Jed, come meet Royce and his buddy, Charles."

Jed warmed immediately to Royce's ready smile and friendly extended hand. "Good to meet you, Jed." Royce nodded at the shorter man by his side. "This is Charles. We work for the same law firm in LA, and this is his first time on a ranch."

Charles' grey eyes coolly appraised Jed, taking in all of him from head to toe with that one look, and Jed felt he'd just been examined, judged and perhaps dismissed as dispensable. But the smile that played about Charles' mouth belied the action, and his proffered hand was warm and firm in Jed's grasp.

"Are you a real cowboy, like Parker?" Charles asked, mischief dancing in his eyes.

"Uh, yeah. I guess I am." Jed felt strangely tongue-tied under that keen gaze. *This one could be trouble,* he thought. *The kind of trouble I can never handle.* Pulling himself together, he added, "Stick around and you might see for yourself."

Any smart reply Charles might have given was curtailed by Aaron's shout of welcome for his son. Charles smiled as father and son embraced, and Charles was struck by their physical resemblance to one another. *Easy to see where Royce got his good looks.*

"Dad, this is Charles."

Charles had to hold back a wince as Aaron grabbed his hand in a hard calloused grip and shook it hard. "Nice to meet you, son. Welcome to the Double R. Royce, why don't you show Charlie his room then we can all meet in the kitchen? Annie's fixin' a spread for you."

"Oh, but we stopped for lunch—"

Aaron narrowed his eyes at Royce. "Then you'd better get ready to eat some more, 'cause I ain't about to tell Annie you're not hungry after the trouble she went to."

Royce laughed. "Okay, Dad, got the picture. We can go for a long hike after."

"Whatever," Aaron grunted. "Jed, Parker—got some things to go over with you both in my office. We'll see you in a few minutes, Royce—and you, Charlie."

Charles didn't want to tell Aaron just then that he wasn't into being called Charlie. Later, he might drop him a hint. He followed Royce up the wide wooden staircase that led to the second story of the big house.

"Your dad's nice," he commented.

"He's the best," Royce said. "He's been terrific since he found out about Parker and me. He might not think it's the greatest thing that could've happened, but he's been supportive of us both. I know he thinks the world of Parker. Here you go, Charles, this is your room. We had it painted a couple of months ago to brighten it up some."

"Very nice," Charles said, looking around. "I think I shall be very happy here, sir."

"Dump your bag, and I'll show you my room. It's right next door."

"So how do you and Parker manage to have, you know, *sex*, when you're here. Is your dad okay with it?"

Royce chuckled as he opened the door to his room and waved Charles inside. "It's easier when Parker comes to LA, of course, but we manage here. Parker's the one who's more discreet than I am. He won't touch me when Dad's in the room, and one time when I kissed him, just on the cheek mind, in front of Dad, he really told me off later. He's more old-fashioned than my father."

"He's a sweetie—and you're one very lucky guy." Charles walked to the window and looked out at the acres of land surrounding the house. "A room with a view—very romantic."

"What did you think of Jed?"

"Hot. I like a man with wide shoulders, but there's a sad soul in there." Charles shivered. "Too much going on for a whore like me to deal with."

"You're not a whore, Charles." Royce grinned at his friend. "You just like to sample all that life has to offer."

Charles sighed. "And you'd think that after all that sampling, I'd have come up with something worthwhile."

"Why don't you get to know Jed better? He might just be worthwhile. Parker says he thinks Jed's the steadfast kind."

"Does he know him that well?"

"Not well, but Parker's pretty intuitive about people. They met a of years ago at a rodeo in Wyoming. Hit it off right away, Parker said. Jed was working a ranch in Cattle Valley. Heard of it?"

"No, should I?"

"Well, it's almost entirely a gay community."

"You're kidding me. Full of gay cowboys?"

"Pretty much."

"I'll have to ask my travel agent to book me a of weeks there soon as we get back to LA."

Royce chuckled. "Well, you've got one right here at the Double R."

"Yeah, but like I said, there's too much going on inside his head."

* * * *

Later, as they all sat around the kitchen table laden with Annie's delicious spread of ham and roast beef sandwiches, piles of fresh fruit, and a home-baked cake consisting of several layers separated by chocolate cream,

Charles' comment on Jed seemed to be right on. The man hardly said a word and had a hard time coming up with answers to any questions thrown his way. When Charles tried to bring up the subject of Cattle Valley — after all, in his opinion, it was one of the most interesting things he heard about all day — Jed's expression clouded, and it was obvious to Charles he'd pretended not to hear, simply tucking in to yet another sandwich.

The man could eat, Charles noticed, or was he just using it as a defence — refusing to speak with his mouth full? A nice mouth, Charles also noticed — wide, with a full lower lip just right for kissing. A kissable mouth. Charles felt his cock twitch at the thought of Jed's mouth on his — *sans* the sandwich, of course.

Nice eyes too, Charles mused. *A kind of hazely-green. When he looks up and the sunlight hits him, there's little flecks of darker green in there. Beautiful really... He really is a honey. Wonder if that rusty hair goes all the way down.*

"So, what you boys got planned for the rest of the day?" Aaron asked, pouring himself a cup of coffee. He waved the pot at Charles. "Charlie — how about you?"

"No thanks, Mr. Chandler."

"Aaron, it's Aaron, Charlie. No need to be so formal."

"And it's Ch — Charlie's just fine." Charles figured it would be just a bit rude to correct Aaron at that point. Maybe later.

"I thought we'd take Charles riding," Royce said. "He's ridden a horse before, so it won't be a problem."

Charles stayed quiet. He'd lied about that, not wanting to appear too much the city slicker. His dad had tried to put him on a horse when he was ten — and he'd shrieked when he'd seen how far off the ground he was. Now at age twenty-nine, surely he could handle it better? God help him if he shrieked!

"Uh, well, it's been a while, Royce," he mumbled.

"Don't worry," Parker said. "I've got you a nice filly with no attitude."

"Oh, great..."

* * * *

Amazing himself, Charles didn't shriek, nor did he fall off the pretty horse Parker had chosen for him. He actually ended up having a really good time, even if Jed's company was no more entertaining than at the kitchen table.

Morose was Charles' opinion of the man after taking several furtive glances at his handsome profile as they rode side by side. Royce had asked Jed to accompany them. "Good way to get a feel of the place," he used as an excuse, though Charles knew Royce was trying to set him and Jed up. Too bad there was absolutely no chance in hell of that happening. The man was just too *morose*. Charles did find himself wondering just what could have been so bad in his life to make him look and act that way. A lost love, he decided. If Jed was as steadfast as Parker considered him to be, then a bad ending to a love affair would most likely hit him hard.

After they returned, had stabled the horses, and Jed had taken his leave, making his way to the bunkhouse, Charles asked, "Did he ever give you a reason for leaving Cattle Valley? Seems to me it's the ideal place for a gay cowboy."

"Personal reasons was all he'd say," Parker told him. "I did hear through the gossip mill that cowboys are famous for, believe it or not, that he'd had some kind of falling out with one of the other ranch hands."

"Aha, that's what I thought," Charles said, watching Jed's tall frame disappear inside the bunkhouse.

"So, here's your chance, Charles." Royce rubbed his friend's back encouragingly. "You could supply the shoulder he needs to cry on."

"No thank you. Been there, done that, and there is no reward at the end of the shoulder supplying. Seven times out of ten, they feel much better and go off to make the same damned mistake all over again, and the other three get all embarrassed and won't talk to you again. And my gut feeling is that Jed is the one out of three kind. If he ever opened up to me or anyone else, he'd most likely never be able to look me in the eye again."

"You think so?" Royce asked as they walked back to the ranch house. "I think he's a lonely soul and needs someone to talk to."

"Well," Charles said, "I sure hope he finds someone — and that, my darling Royce, is the end of my involvement on the topic of Jed."

Chapter Three

Annie had prepared a dinner fit for kings, and surprisingly, both Royce and Charles did it justice.

"Must be all this fresh air," Charles said, patting his stomach and sipping at his red wine. "I haven't eaten this much in years."

"Annie always spoils me when I come home," Royce remarked, smiling across the table at Parker. It was obvious to Charles that Royce and Parker would be making their excuses at any moment. Well, it *had* been a long day…

Aaron yawned mightily. "I'm turnin' in, boys. I'll leave you to entertain each other. Goodnight."

Royce got up to hug his dad. "G'night, Dad." Charles saw his face redden after Aaron had whispered something in his ear.

Charles couldn't resist asking after Aaron left the room, "What'd he say? Don't make too much noise?"

Royce chuckled. "How did you guess? That should have been a buzz-kill, but Parker and me have been too long apart for it to slow us down. Right, Parker?"

Parker gave them both his slow grin. "Right." He pushed himself away from the table. "G'night, Charles. We'll do some more ridin' tomorrow. You'll be a seasoned cowhand by the time you leave here."

Charles laughed as he accepted Parker and Royce's hugs. He watched them leave the dining room hand in hand and couldn't quite stop the tug of envy that gripped the pit of his stomach. He might joke about 'sampling all that life has to offer', but he had to admit, each time he saw Royce and Parker so *together,* it almost made him long for some stability in his own life.

He wasn't quite ready to turn in—at least not on his own, and the chances of him finding someone to share his bed around this place were remote indeed. All these hot men, and all terminally straight—except Parker, and he was taken, and Jed, and he was way too moody and fucked-up at the moment. Charles felt sorry for the guy. Maybe some hot sex could take Jed's mind of his woes, but all that baggage—ugh.

Maybe if Charles went for a walk it would tire him out some.

He wandered out from the front porch, walking slowly so he could look up at the star-filled night sky. Charles was originally from a small town outside Madison, Wisconsin. As a boy, his dad had taken him on fishing and camping trips which he'd hated, but he remembered with a sort of reluctant fondness the times he and his father had lain under starry skies, his father pointing out the various constellations and quietly murmuring their names. Since living in Los Angeles, Charles hadn't seen too many starry skies, the lights of the city only serving to illuminate the ever-present layer of yellow haze overhead.

He stopped to take in the wonders above him — the North Star, the Big Dipper, Orion, and the brilliant patterns his father had named for him all those years ago.

"Hi there."

Startled, Charles swung round at the sound of the voice behind him. Jed stood there, looming over him, weaving as if he stood on a storm-tossed boat instead of the solid earth of the Double R. Charles gazed up at him, bemused.

"Now, ain't you the cutest thing," Jed slurred, reaching for him.

Charles took a step back. "Excuse me?"

"I said —"

"I heard what you said, Jed. You said, 'Ain't you the cutest thing' — or was it thang? You can take that corny cowboy parlance and shove it. You're drunk as a skunk and should go lie down."

Jed weaved some more, his arms hanging uselessly by his sides. He lurched forward suddenly, barrelling into Charles with such force they both ended up on the hard ground.

"Ouch!" Charles pushed at the big body lying on top of him. "Get off me, you freakin' idiot." He stiffened as a choking sound came from Jed's throat. Charles pushed at him again without success. "Don't you dare throw up on me!"

But Jed didn't move, and Charles had to squirm his way from under the long, hard body that covered him. In the process, Jed rolled over onto his back, moaning out loud.

"Shut up, and *get up*," Charles hissed, glaring down at Jed. "There's no way I can lift you — get up."

"Can't..."

"Yes, you can. Now get *up*!"

"Jus' lee me...be fine."

"Oh, for heaven's sake." Charles looked around in the vain hope someone might show up to help him get the cowboy on his feet. He could go get Parker, but he and Royce were most likely in the land of ecstasy right about now and surely wouldn't appreciate Charles asking for help with a stretched out drunk.

Royce's dad? No, bad idea. He'd probably fire Jed's ass for getting drunk on only his second night at the Double R.

Charles knelt by Jed's side. "Jed, you have to get up."

His eyes roamed over the tall man's hard, slim body. His shirt was open showing a smooth expanse of tanned flesh. Unable to resist, Charles pushed his hand under the cotton fabric and gently stroked Jed's chest, lingering over one nipple that pebbled under his touch.

He studied the cowboy's face, the thick lashes that dusted his prominent cheekbones, the long straight nose, the wide mouth now slightly open as if waiting to be kissed. He touched the cleft on Jed's chin then ran his thumb over the full lower lip.

"You really are one beautiful man," he murmured. "Drunken idiot that you are."

"Feel's nice."

Charles met Jed's bleary-eyed gaze. "You can't lie here, Jed. Come on. If I give you a hand, do you think you could stand?"

"Try..."

"Okay." Charles got to his feet, giving a furtive stroke over the growing bulge in his chinos. Damn, just one brief feel of the man's body, and he was hard. He got behind Jed, who was trying to sit up. He slid his arms under Jed's armpits and encircled his chest. "Okay, on three, stand up. One, two, *three!*" Charles heaved, and amazingly Jed was on his feet, unsteady, but standing.

"Good. Now put your arm around my shoulders, and I'll try to get you to your room."

"Too far," Jed mumbled. "Barn'll do."

"Jeez, you really are a hayseed, aren't you?"

"If you say so."

Charles chuckled and tightened his arm around Jed's waist. "Okay, big boy, the barn it is—but don't scare the horses." Together they staggered over to the barn. Charles pulled on the door handle. Locked. *Great.* "It's locked."

"Key's under that slab, 'case of 'mergencies."

"Okay, lean on the door 'til I get it." He waited until Jed had supported himself against the barn door then knelt to pull the key from under the concrete slab. Quickly, he unlocked the door, hauled it open slightly and tried to push Jed inside.

"Y'come too—"

Charles sighed but entered the barn behind Jed who reached for him, leaning heavily on his shoulders.

They walked a few steps then Jed muttered, "This'll do," before falling face down on a pile of straw.

"Oh, for—you can't lie like that. You'll suffocate."

Jed made some kind of incoherent reply but didn't move.

"Roll over, you giant pain in the ass." Charles knelt by him, pushing at his shoulder. "Move!"

Groaning, Jed rolled onto his back, one arm hooked over Charles' back. He opened his eyes. "You're s'cute."

"Ain't I though." Despite himself, Charles smiled into Jed's eyes. Jed applied pressure to Charles' back and pulled him in close. Charles gasped as their lips touched, and Jed's warm, whisky scented breath filled his mouth. "We shouldn't do this," he whispered against the soft full flesh of Jed's lower lip.

"Know—but nice."

"Yes, it is—even nicer than nice." Charles knew he would regret this in the morning, especially the moment when Jed would look at him without any memory of what had taken place between them. But oh, the cowboy looked and felt so good, and if it never happened again, at least he had this moment to remember. His mind reeled as Jed's mouth covered his, his tongue seeking and gaining entrance to the moist warmth beyond Charles' parted lips. Charles sucked on Jed's tongue, holding it captive for a moment or two, making Jed moan and pull Charles even tighter against him. Their bodies writhed together and Charles could feel the thick hard ridge between Jed's thighs. He wanted desperately to see it, to hold it, to kiss it and watch it swell to its maximum length, which he was sure would be more than just impressive. He struggled to free himself from Jed's arms.

"Where you goin'?"

"Nowhere, cowboy. I'm staying right here with you."

"Tha's good."

Charles sat astride Jed's thighs, smiling down at him as he unbuckled the thick leather belt around Jed's hips. "Lift up, cowboy." And Jed complied, lifting his butt off the straw so that Charles could ease his jeans down, revealing his bulging briefs.

"Oh, yeah…" Charles lowered his head and ran his lips over the thick length that throbbed under the white cotton. He heard Jed's breath catch in his throat, felt rough hands tousle his hair, stroke his face. He turned one side of his face into the calloused palm, almost purring from the sensation of Jed's fingers caressing the soft skin under his ear. He nuzzled the head of Jed's cock that had just poked its way from under the elastic of Jed's briefs. Charles lapped at the juice spilling from it, and Jed's body bucked from the feel of Charles' tongue on his flesh.

"Charlie," Jed gasped, and Charles froze in mid-lick. Another one calling him Charlie — Jeez! But hey, what the hell did it matter what Jed called him right now? He was so obviously into what *Charlie* was doing, he might just remember it all when he woke from his drunken stupor. Charles pulled Jed's cock free of his briefs and licked it from base to tip and back down again, his tongue gliding over Jed's balls, taking each one between his lips, rolling them gently in his mouth, causing Jed to moan out loud and his body to thrash in ecstasy against the straw he lay on.

"Yeah, baby," Charles murmured then went back to giving Jed's cock the attention it craved. Grasping it at the base, he swirled his tongue over the swollen head then brought as much of it into his mouth as he could. He had to really open wide to accommodate its thickness. His lips slid down the length until the head lodged in his throat where his muscles constricted around it squeezing even more pre-cum from the slit. A long groan escaped Jed's lips, and his body spasmed under Charles.

"Gonna come," he gasped. "*Charlie.*"

Charles sucked long and hard, his lips and tongue swirling over and laving every glorious, throbbing inch of Jed's cock. The cowboy's moans grew in volume until Charles was sure everybody on the ranch would be heading for the barn wondering who was being murdered. Then with a choking cry Jed came, filling Charles' mouth and throat with his salty cream, his body vibrating with the intensity of his orgasm. Charles held him in his mouth until he had calmed and every last drop was wrested from him.

A long sigh was wrenched from Jed as he collapsed back into the straw. One hand stroked Charles' hair, once, twice then stilled. Charles drew himself up over Jed's leanly muscled torso and kissed his lips gently. He chuckled ruefully as a soft snore emanated from Jed's slightly parted lips. Not surprisingly, the cowboy was out cold. Well, any further ravaging was going to have to wait for another day or night, if ever. Jed was in no condition to reciprocate. Charles gazed down at Jed's face, wondering if he would remember any of what has happened when he awoke.

Probably not. He might remember something, but the *somebody* was another thing entirely. Charles kissed Jed's cheek, gently smoothed back the copper coloured hair that had tumbled over his forehead then lingered over his lips again. Such beautiful lips... With a sigh, he buttoned Jed's shirt, slipped his still semi-erect cock back into his briefs, buttoned his fly, and arranged his belt loosely back into place. At least now, if anyone came into the barn before Jed woke, they wouldn't find him with his clothes in disarray and his cock hanging out.

Charles stood, and for a long moment, he remained, simply looking down at Jed and wishing—and oh, such a dumb wish really, he told himself—wishing that Jed would remember every moment and tell him, in the morning, how much he'd loved it, and could they do it again right away? A wry smile twisted Charles' lips as he turned to go. He looked back for just a moment at Jed's inert figure sprawled on top of the straw then he slipped through the slightly open barn door and made his way back to the ranch house.

Chapter Four

Royce woke up smiling. This had become a habit since he and Parker had been sleeping together and waking up together. Feeling the warmth and hard muscle of Parker's body spooning his made Royce happier than he'd thought he ever could be. He pushed his butt into Parker's crotch eliciting a groan from his lover.

"Again?" came the muffled voice, warm lips moving on Royce's shoulder.

"Are you complaining, old man?"

Parker snorted. "I'm only a year older than you, darlin', and can take you anytime."

Royce turned to face his lover. "You got that right." He pressed his lips to Parker's. "So take me now."

"I have to pee first."

Royce slapped Parker's muscular butt. "Then go pee, and come back with it even harder than it is now."

"What a slave driver you are." Parker rolled out of bed then bent to kiss Royce's cheek. "Shouldn't you check on your buddy? I think I just heard him go downstairs."

"Do I have to? What happened to you taking me?"

"Okay, but we should make it a quickie. You have to play a nice host."

"So the quicker you pee and get back here and have our quickie, the quicker I'll be playing nice host to Charles."

"Got it." Parker grinned at him and hurried into the bathroom.

* * * *

Charles could smell the delicious aroma of fresh coffee coming from the kitchen. Annie and Aaron sat at the table enjoying their first cup of the day.

"Charlie…" Aaron beamed at him. "You're an early riser, huh? No sign of Royce yet?"

"Uh, no, but I expect he'll be down in a minute." *Or going down in a minute.*

"You sleep all right?" Annie asked. "I know a strange bed can be difficult first night."

"Like a log," Charles lied, remembering how he'd tossed restlessly after his encounter with Jed. *Wonder how* he *feels this morning.*

"Have some coffee, son," Aaron said, pulling the chair next him out from under the table. "Take a load off."

"Thanks." Charles sat and took the coffee mug Annie pushed in front of him.

"So, what d'you think of this neck of the woods, Charlie?" Aaron looked at him keenly. "Think you could live around here?"

"Huh?" The question took Charles by surprise.

"Well, I know Royce is thinking of opening his own office here one of these days, and he did mention your name as partner."

"Oh, yeah." Charles sipped his coffee. "Mmm, good. Yes, we've talked about it, but it might be another year or so. I've been to Sacramento before, and I like it okay. If Royce plans on going ahead, I'd be glad to join him."

"Good, good. That's swell. I know Parker will be happier than a dog with two tails when Royce is up here full time. They're planning on gettin' their own spread you know."

Charles smiled. "You are a really nice man, Mr Chandler, I mean, Aaron. Not too many fathers would be as accepting as you are."

"Huh," Annie huffed. "Don't let him fool you. If he hadn't been lying helpless in a hospital bed when Royce and Parker made up their differences, he'd never have had a clue."

Charles chuckled. "Yes, I heard about that."

"Well, it was one way of finding out, I guess," Aaron said gruffly. "They're good boys though, both of 'em."

"Yes, they are," Annie agreed. She leant across the table, fixing Charles with an earnest gaze. "So, what do you think of Jed?"

Again, Charles found himself surprised by a question he hadn't expected. "Um, Jed?"

"Yes, the new hand. He's gay you know. Just wondered if you'd figured what was bugging him."

"Now, Annie," Aaron protested. "How in hell could you expect Charlie to know the answer to that? He only met the man yesterday."

"*I* only met him day before yesterday," Annie said, "and I could tell right away he's a lonesome soul. Lot on his mind, that one."

You're right about that, Charles thought. "I think he'll be fine once he settles in and gets busy on the ranch."

"That's right," Aaron said. "Nothing like hard work to take your mind off your troubles. I'll make sure he's got no time on his hands for brooding."

"Who's brooding?" Royce asked as he entered the kitchen. "'Morning all. Annie, coffee smells great."

"Sit, I'll pour you a mug."

"We were talking about Jed," Charles informed him. "Annie thinks he's a lonesome soul. What do you think, Royce?"

Royce shrugged. "He's quiet, that's for sure. A thinker, maybe."

"Where's Parker?" Aaron asked.

"In the shower," Royce replied, picking up his coffee mug. "Says he's got a big day planned, or rather what you planned for him and Jed, Dad."

Aaron chuckled. "Yep. Kinda loading them up today. They'll be back before dinnertime, I expect. I'll tell Parker to have Jed join us. Make him feel welcome."

Great, Charles thought. *Now I get to watch him avoiding my eyes across the dinner table all night.*

The sound of clattering boots on wooden stairs announced Parker's arrival. "Mornin' Boss, everyone—"

Royce jumped up to pour him a mug of coffee, and once again, Charles felt that little tug of envy just seeing how close the two men were. He gave an involuntary sigh. He really had to stop wasting his life on one-night stands or drunk-ass cowboys. Well, in truth, Jed had been his first cowboy—real cowboy that is. There had been that guy from Texas in a Stetson one Halloween.

"Wanna go riding again today, Charles?" Royce asked him.

"There's a few stray cows we need bringin' in from up in the north quarter," Aaron said, winking at Royce. "You could show Charlie how it's done. Send him back to LA a real cowboy."

"What do you say, Charles?" Royce's green eyes were shining with expectancy. "Sound like fun?"

Charles couldn't think of anything that might be less fun, but it was obvious Royce was eager to go. "Sounds like a lot of fun," he said. "Let's get to it!"

* * * *

Jed, standing by the corral, waiting for Parker to start their day together, pressed a hand to his throbbing temple and mentally called himself all kinds of a fool. What had he been thinking about, getting soused like that last night? If old man Chandler had seen him drunk as a skunk, he'd have fired his ass for sure. He could thank his lucky stars that Royce's buddy had been the only one to see him in that state.

Charlie. Funny thing, he couldn't remember getting back to the ranch. That had been really dumb—driving in the condition he'd been in. He couldn't really remember how he and Charlie had ended up in the barn together either. *Guess I told him not to take me to my room – wonder why?* But he sure as hell remembered every other thing that had happened. That guy could surely suck cock. It had been amazing. Just thinking about it made him hard, just like it had when he'd wakened in the morning flat on his back on a pile of straw in the barn. Charlie had been the first thing that had popped into his mind when he'd opened his eyes and stared up at the barn's wooden roof. He'd half hoped Charlie had still been there, lying next to him.

It would have been nice to cuddle some, maybe even do it all again. The guy had even covered him up before he'd left. Spared him embarrassment if someone had come into the barn early. Nice guy, Charlie. And Jed had been sure the little fella hadn't even liked him much.

He'd have to find a subtle way of thanking him for looking after him, for not leaving him lying in the dirt, and for — well, might be kinda hard to say 'Thanks for the blow-job'. Maybe, just 'Thanks for everything'. He couldn't quite remember if Charlie had taken his clothes off. No, he'd surely remember that. He bet Charlie's body would be good to see. It had been good to hold — what he could remember.

"'Morning, Jed." Parker's cheery voice brought Jed out of his reverie.

"Oh, 'mornin' Parker. You got our schedule from the boss-man?"

"Yep, right here. We'll take the truck into town first and pick up the supplies he asked for. Then there's that acreage he wants us to look at. We can do that on the way back."

"Sounds good."

"You sleep all right last night?" Parker asked. "You look a mite weary."

"Stayed up too late."

"Well, tomorrow's Sunday. No early chores, so you can sleep in." He slapped Jed on the back. "Let's go."

* * * *

From his bedroom window, Charles watched Jed and Parker climb into the truck and take off in a cloud of dust. Well, at least, he wouldn't have to deal with any averted looks until dinner. Too bad, really. He wondered what would have happened if Jed hadn't been drunk, and they'd just met casually in the moonlight, instead of Jed falling on him in a drunken stupor. Would either one of them suggested they go for a little stroll? Would they have ended up in the barn anyway in each other's arms? Would what they started last night have gone further? Charles shivered and his ass muscles clenched at the thought of Jed's beautiful hard cock pushing its way between his butt cheeks and filling him with its amazing girth.

Hmm. Was there any possible way he could get the cowboy alone again? Unlikely, he knew, but Charles had been in unlikely situations before when he'd thought *not a chance*, and then by some twist of fate, some stroke of luck, or maybe the fact the other guy had been drunk, they had connected. Oh no, he wasn't going to go that route. Getting Jed drunk, even if he could, would defeat the purpose of the exercise. No, he wanted Jed sober and willing—and eager to go all the way.

He turned from the window at the knock on his door. Royce poked his blond head round the corner. "Ready?"

"Always," Charles replied, picking up his billfold from the dresser and slipping it into his jeans pocket.

"You're not going to need that, you know," Royce told him.

"No? I thought we might stop off at a Starbucks later."

"Funny guy," Royce said, ruffling Charles' hair.

"Oh, right, forgot—we're in Brokeback Mountain territory."

"That was in Wyoming, Charles."

"Right again. Where all the gay cowboys are—can we ride over there?"

* * * *

"Something happened last night," Charles said as he and Royce sat astride their mounts and watched a of stray cows grazing peacefully, unaware of the men's presence.

"Oh, yeah?"

"You can't tell anyone, not even Parker, and definitely not your dad."

"What the heck did you do?"

"I'm only telling you this 'cause I'm going to need your help."

"*Charles*, what did you do?"

"I sucked Jed off last night."

"*What*?" Royce's expression was a picture of incredulity. "How did you manage that?"

"He was drunk—that's why I don't want Parker or Aaron to know. I don't want to get him in trouble."

Royce chuckled. "Jed isn't the first of our hands to get drunk."

"I know, but it was his first day on the job, and all that, and it might not go down too well. And truth to tell, and I know this is going to sound funny coming from me—I kinda like the guy."

"You said he was morose and had too much baggage. What made you change your mind?"

Charles sighed. "I don't know, there was just something about him, last night. Something vulnerable, sweet, affectionate—different."

"Wow. How was his dick?'

"*Royce*."

"Oh come on, Charles. Enquiring minds need to know."

"Why is it every gay guy has to know dick size? As if that was any judge of the man's character."

Royce exploded with laughter. "Oh, my — will the real Charles Fletcher please put his hand up? I don't know who this person is, sitting on a horse next to me."

"Oh, all right. I know this doesn't sound like me, and maybe I'm having an aneurysm or something, but I really feel like I want to get to know him better. What makes him tick — what makes him seem so sad. When we were, uh, doing it, he was like a different person."

"You said you needed my help," Royce reminded him.

"Yeah, somehow I have to get him alone. Not cornered or anything — just him and me, alone together."

"He does have his own room."

"I know, but I can't just go barging over there, now can I?"

"Well, I could take you over to see Parker's room. We had all the rooms redecorated recently — that might work as an excuse."

"Yeah, queens love to exchange decorating secrets. He's just gonna love to hear me squealing with delight over your choice of comforter."

Royce laughed. "Who said you had to squeal? Save that for later."

"Okay. So you take me over to Parker's room. How does that get me into Jed's?"

"We'll think of something when we're there. I could just say, 'Oh, Jed, why don't you show Charles your room while we're here?'

"Ouch." Charles shuddered visibly. "That is the worst line I've ever heard."

"Well, you think of something. I'll get you over there then you're on your own. Now come on, we have to round up those li'l doggies!"

Charles rolled his eyes. "I might just throw up."

* * * *

Dinner had been announced for six o'clock, and it was almost five when Royce and Charles arrived back at the ranch, complete with three 'doggies'. Charles' ass ached from prolonged saddle use, and he couldn't wait to get in the shower. As they walked from the stable to the house, Parker's truck swung in through the gates and came to a screeching halt in front of them.

"Royce, Charles, give us a hand here," Parker yelled, jumping down from the truck. "We got a shitload of supplies to unload. Jed, see if you can round up a couple of of the guys to help."

Charles tried to keep his face expressionless as Jed strode towards him, but as the other man smiled shyly at him, he couldn't help but break out in a big grin. *He smiled at me—he remembers!* Charles swivelled on his feet to watch Jed as he walked quickly to the bunkhouse, and took a long moment to admire the shapely butt between the narrow hips that swayed with a sensuous yet masculine grace. It took all of Charles' self control not to run after Jed and ask him point blank if he could see him later in the evening.

Pull yourself together and stop acting like a dizzy teenager, he told himself, dragging his gaze away from Jed and hurrying to help Royce and Parker unload the truck. *All he did was smile, for Chrissakes. He could have been simply apologising for being drunk. The rest he might not remember at all.*

When Jed returned with another ranch hand, Parker thanked Royce and Charles and said they'd manage the rest.

"Good, I need to shower," Royce said. "I smell more like a horse than the horse does!"

Charles, after a quick sniff at his armpits, agreed, and the two of them hurried into the house, and to their separate rooms to shower. Charles spent a long time under the spray, working up a good lather all over, but especially on his crotch and up his butt crack. If, and it was still a big 'if' he and Jed connected again tonight, he wanted to smell clean and fresh down there. Once he'd dressed, choosing a light blue polo shirt and tan slacks, he searched his toilet bag for something he hadn't thought he might need on this particular trip.

Ah yes, there it was—the small foil wrapper that he now carefully stowed in his back pocket. *Hey*, he thought, checking his reflection in the mirror one last time, *you never know!*

* * * *

Royce, soaping Parker's back in the shower, tickled his lover's ear with his lips then whispered, "Charles and Jed did the nasty last night."

Parker's head swung round in surprise. "Together?"

"Of course together, silly." Royce slipped his soapy fingers between Parker's ass cheeks. "Charles didn't want you to know 'cause Jed was drunk, and he thought you'd be mad at him—at Jed, that is. So don't act as if you know, and you have to help me get them together again tonight."

"Can't they do that themselves?" Parker shivered as Royce's fingers probed at his opening. "And if you keep that up we're gonna be late for Annie's cookin'."

Royce sighed and withdrew his fingers. He wrapped his arms around Parker's chest and held him close, his lips gliding over the nape of Parker's neck.

"I think it'd be cool if Charles and Jed got to know one another better. Jed seems so sad, don't you think? What did you guys talk about on your trip today?"

"Stuff. You know me, I don't like to pry into other folk's affairs."

"Aren't you just a teeny bit curious about him? Charles said he was totally different when they were doing, you know…"

Parker chuckled. "All of us are different when we're doin' *you know*." He turned off the shower spray and turned to face Royce. He kissed his lips tenderly. "Okay, Mr. Matchmaker, what do you have in mind?"

"Well, Charles wasn't crazy about me taking him over to the bunkhouse to show him your room—and Jed's, if we asked nice."

Parker grimaced. "Sounds kinda contrived." He opened the shower door and reached for a towel then began drying Royce's chest.

"Of course, it's contrived," Royce said, "but it's the best I could come up with."

"Well, let me think about it. Maybe I can get Jed and Charles interested in something."

"Like what?"

"I dunno." He kissed Royce's lips lightly. "Let me think on it!"

Chapter Five

Parker brought Jed up to the house a few minutes before six, and Aaron immediately plied them with his favourite drink—Old Tawny. Charles watched with interest as Jed shook his head and asked if he might have a beer instead.

Good, he thought, *he's playing it safe tonight. But it might not be a bad idea if he got just a little looser. Looks hot, too. That shirt and those jeans look like a second skin on him.* As Royce and Parker kept Aaron busy in conversation, Jed smiled at Charles and crossed the room to where he stood by the fireplace.

"I want to say thanks for last night," Jed said quietly, his eyes gleaming.

"Thanks? It was my pleasure," Charles told him, returning his smile.

"Well, you know, I was kinda drunk."

"Kinda?" Charles chuckled. "That's an understatement if I ever heard one. I'm amazed you remember anything about last night."

Jed's face flushed. "I don't do that very often."

"I hope not—and I especially hope you don't drive in that condition very often."

Jed frowned. "I didn't come over here so you could lecture me."

Charles bit his lip. "Sorry. Of course, it's none of my business what you do. I'm just saying it's not a good idea to drink and drive."

The warmth had vanished from Jed's eyes. "That's what they say, all right. I'll have to remember that in the future." He turned to go.

Charles put a hand on his arm. "Jed, I'm sorry. That came out wrong. What I meant was I'd be worried if you got into an accident or something."

Jed gave him a long look, his eyes searching Charles'. "Yeah, it was kinda dumb of me to be driving the way I was." He looked down at his feet, for a moment, then his hazel gaze locked on Charles. "Anyway, I was wondering…"

"Yes?"

Jed cleared his throat. "If you'd like to…"

"Dinner's on the table, gents. Come and get it!" Annie's jovial voice stopped Jed in mid sentence.

"Go on," Charles said.

"Come on, Jed 'n Charles," Annie yelled. "Guests of honour with me, pronto!"

Jed turned to follow her, and Charles, grinding his teeth in frustration, had no option but to tag along behind. He glared at Royce as he passed. "He was just about to—"

Aaron grabbed Charles's arm. "Come on, Charlie. You'll sit by me, and we'll get drunk together."

Oh, boy. Charles ground his teeth some more.

"You'll do no such thing, Aaron Chandler," Annie said over her shoulder as she led Jed into the dining room. "Keep that gut-poison off my table until you've eaten every single thing I put in front of you!"

Behind them Charles heard Royce and Parker chuckle. "That's told you, Dad!"

"Damned woman thinks she owns the place," Aaron muttered. "So what are we drinkin' with dinner?" he asked, frowning at his housekeeper.

"I had Parker pick us up some fancy wine that Charles will approve of, I'm sure. Now Jed, you sit here. Charles, you'll be opposite Jed. Aaron, you're head of the table, Royce, the other end, Parker you best sit next to Royce, and I'll sit up there with the old man."

"Bossy old woman," Aaron, mumbled.

"Can I help?" Charles asked her.

"Heavens no, darlin'. You're a guest, and I'm used to doing this. Raised three sons and a daughter, you know." With that she swept off into the kitchen while the men took their places at the table.

Charles smiled across at Jed and felt his blood run hot as Jed smiled back at him. Their eyes met and held, and Charles knew with a clear certainty that his buddy Royce had no need to arrange any bunkhouse viewings.

* * * *

After dinner, and after Annie had graciously accepted the accolades heaped on her with regard to her cooking skills, Royce said, "Okay, Annie, now you just go sit and relax with dad. Me, and my friends here, will take care of the washing up."

"I wouldn't dream of it," Annie cried, but Royce and Parker laughingly took her by each arm and made her sit next to Aaron in the parlour. "Okay, boys," Parker said, "let's do it."

The four of them marched into the kitchen and soon laid waste to the piles of plates and pans. Royce and Parker washed, while Jed and Charles shared the drying chore. Several times when Jed passed a plate to Charles their fingers would touch and they would smile at each other. Royce, who was watching them like a hawk, nudged Parker and rolled his eyes their way. Parker just chuckled.

"Anyone feel like a stroll to work off some of that food?" Royce asked when they were done.

"Sounds good," Jed said, looking at Charles.

Charles nodded. "I'm game."

"Why don't you two get a head start then?" Parker suggested. "I just need a word with Aaron before we go. We'll catch you up."

"Oh, okay." Jed touched Charles' arm and headed for the back door.

"That was neat," Royce said as the door closed behind Charles and Jed. He gave Parker a peck on the cheek. "We'll just take our time here."

"That's right. No sense in hurryin' out there, is there?"

* * * *

Charles slowed his footsteps as he turned his face up to the sky to view the stars.

"Pretty, huh?" Jed murmured beside him.

"This is what I was doing when you came upon me last night—stargazing."

"Then I came along in all my drunken assholeyness."

Charles chuckled. "Now, *there's* a word."

Jed kicked at the dirt with the heel of his boot. "I'm glad I don't remember most of that part."

"You mean you don't recall the two of us lying here, you on top of me?"

"Oh, Charlie, for Pete's sake, don't tell me I came onto you out here!"

"You fell on me, out here," Charles said, laughing.

"I am so sorry."

"Don't be." He flashed Jed a mischievous smile. "It was kinda nice, once I'd figured you weren't going to throw up on me."

Jed groaned.

"No, really. You looked…uh, very sweet lying there."

"Charlie, you are embarrassing the hell outta me."

Methinks the cowboy doth protest too much, Charles mused, hiding the smile that played on his lips. He looked back at the house. "Seems our friends aren't too interested in joining us." He tugged at Jed's arm. "Shall we?"

"Well, least in the dark, you can't see my face is redder than a beetroot. Hey—" Jed pointed to where his Jeep was parked. "Wanna take a ride?"

"Should we tell Royce and Parker?"

"Somethin' tells me they don't care what we do."

Though Royce will be full of questions in the morning, Charles thought with a wry smile. "Okay," he said. "Let's go for a moonlight ride. You can tell me your darkest secrets, and I'll tell you mine."

"You have dark secrets, Charlie?" Jed asked as he opened the Jeep door for him.

"Doesn't everyone?"

Jed waited until Charles had seated himself then he leant in and kissed Charles gently on the lips. "I don't think there's very much darkness in you, Charlie."

Charles, surprised by Jed's kiss, stared at him with wide eyes.

"Didn't think so," Jed murmured. He closed the door and walked quickly round to the driver's side.

"So…" Charles grinned at Jed as he slid into his seat. "Now that you've blown my cover, and you know there's absolutely nothing dark and terrible lurking in my background, we'll just have to talk about you."

"Nothing much there either," Jed said, turning the key in the ignition. "Guess we're a really boring pair."

"Or we're both liars."

Jed gave him a sideways glance. "Or that."

* * * *

From the kitchen window Royce watched as Jed's Jeep made its way towards the Double R's gates. He turned and smiled at Parker and put an arm around his lover's waist, pulling him in close.

"Mission accomplished," he whispered.

Parker nodded and laid a kiss on Royce's cheek. "And we didn't have to do a darned thing."

Chapter Six

They drove for some time in silence—not an awkward silence. At least, Charles didn't feel any awkwardness or tension between them.

Then Jed said suddenly, "Can I ask you something?"

"Sure."

"You ever been in love, Charles?"

"Oh, let me think now—wait, you just called me Charles."

"Parker told me you didn't take to bein' called Charlie. I kept waitin' for you to tell me off—you know, like you're kinda good at."

"Lord. You just made me sound like an old nag."

"You're not old," Jed said with a sly smile then laughed and wriggled out of the way as Charles poked him in the ribs. "I'm drivin'!"

Charles let his hand slide down onto Jed's thigh. "I like you this way, Jed. Is that short for something? Jed, I mean."

"Jedediah. My mother was into biblical names. My brother's Saul and my sister's Miriam."

"Miriam's a nice name."

"You don't like Jedediah?"

"It's a bit of a mouthful." Charles squeezed Jed's thigh. "But then, you *are* a bit of a mouthful."

"You're gonna start me blushing again, Charles. And you never answered my question."

"What question?"

"Have you ever been in love?"

"Hundreds of times."

Jed chuckled. "Seriously. Anyone ever left you breathless and pinin' for more?"

"Hundreds of guys."

"Made you so you can't think straight," Jed continued, a wistful smile on his face. "Can't wait to see him again, want to wake up every mornin' with him by your side, live with him, and *for* him only?"

Charles stared at Jed for a long moment before he said quietly, "No, never. I've never felt like that."

Jed turned to stare back at Charles. "Never?"

"Never." Charles let his eyes fall from Jed's gaze. "But you obviously have."

"Why'd you say that?"

"That soul-baring, almost poetic list of emotions you just recited for me," Charles murmured. *"To live with him, and for him only.* Sounds idyllic."

"It was meant to be. I mean, that's what I think love should feel like." Jed slowed the Jeep then drove up onto the shoulder. He turned off the engine and killed the lights. "Wanna get out and walk some?"

"It's dark." Charles peered out through the window. "What if we fall into a ravine or something?"

Jed chuckled. "I'll hold your hand."

Charles jumped out of the Jeep. "Okay, deal."

Still chuckling, Jed came round to Charles' side and took his hand. "The moon's out nice and bright. We won't fall into any ravines."

"Just don't let go of my hand."

They found a fallen tree and sat down together, still holding hands. Charles leaned into Jed who slid and arm around him then kissed the top of his head.

"I like you, Charles. You're different from anyone I've ever known."

"Is that a compliment? Or is that a nice way of saying you've never met anyone as nelly as me?"

"You're not nelly," Jed exclaimed. "I don't think you're nelly. Nelly never entered my mind."

"Okay, okay, I'm not nelly." Charles laughed softly. He craned his neck up trying to reach Jed's mouth. "You're so fucking tall—" He stood and straddled Jed's thighs then wrapped his arms around the tall man's neck. "That's better. Ready for this?"

"You bet." Jed pulled Charles in so their lips met, gently at first then, as Jed gasped, with a fervour that sent Charles' head reeling with desire. His lips parted, and his mouth was filled with Jed's demanding, probing tongue. This cowboy could kiss! Charles fumbled with Jed's shirt buttons, peeling the denim back over wide shoulders then bent to run his lips over the smooth, tanned, pectoral muscles that flexed as Jed leant back in apparent ecstasy. Charles fastened his lips on each tiny brown nipple, the tip of his tongue swirling round the hardening nubs. Jed moaned, leaned farther back—and the two of them toppled off the tree trunk landing on the ground in a tangle of arms and legs.

"Oof—" The air exploded out of Jed's lungs then he laughed, a great shout of undiluted glee, like a happy schoolboy. He hugged Charles to him and kissed him soundly.

"At least, this time you're on top of me," he said, his laughter dying as his lips were worked over by the kiss Charles laid on him. "Boy, but you kiss good."

"So do you, big guy," Charles murmured, tracing Jed's jaw with his lips. He slipped a hand down over Jed's torso to the hard bulge between his legs. "We going to stay here on the ground or take this somewhere else?"

"Back of the Jeep's got some room if I push the seats forward."

"Let's go."

Charles took time to admire Jed's long lean frame as he busied himself pushing first one seat forward then the other. Each time he bent over to find the release lever, Charles let out a low wolf whistle in appreciation of the cowboy's fine ass. Jed chuckled, and he was all smiles as he joined Charles at the back of the Jeep.

"Like what you see?" he teased.

"Like and want," Charles said, pulling at Jed's shirt, freeing it from his jeans then pressing his lips to the warm hard flesh.

"Your turn," Jed murmured, slipping his hands under Charles' polo shirt and lifting it up over his head. Charles raised his arms to help, and Jed leaned in to nuzzle Charles' armpits and inhale his fresh scent.

"No fair!" Charles' muffled voice cried out plaintively. "Get this stupid shirt off my head!"

Chuckling, Jed saved Charles from suffocating then planted a scorching kiss on his mouth. Their bodies pressed tightly together, the sizzling effect of Jed's bare skin on his took Charles' breath away. Jed lifted Charles into the back of the Jeep then crawled in after him.

"Want you naked," he said, tugging Charles' slacks open. He pulled them down, taking Charles' bikini briefs at the same time. "Sweet," he murmured, burying his face in Charles' crotch, inhaling the scent of his musk, his tongue swiping roughly over the head of Charles' engorged cock.

Delirious, Charles tugged impatiently at Jed's belt buckle. "Want you naked, too."

Jed knocked Charles' hand out of the way.

"Easier if I do it," he said, unbuckling himself and wriggling out of his tight jeans and boots. Kicking everything out of the way, he fell on Charles, scooping him into his arms, his mouth scouring Charles' torso, leaving not one inch unkissed.

Charles writhed under him, crying out when the heat of Jed's mouth enveloped him. His body arched in ecstasy, driving his erection into the depths of Jed's throat. Jed grasped Charles' cock at the base, pumping it in and out of his mouth, his lips clamped tightly around the hard flesh, his tongue laving the head, inducing a steady flow of pre-cum from the slit. Jed moved his hand from Charles' cock to his butt, cupping it, pulling him in even deeper until his nose was buried in the curly pubic hair at the root.

His hands clutching at Jed's broad shoulders, Charles was doing his best to hold back, but the insistent tug of

Jed's lips and tongue on his now aching erection proved too much.

"Jed, oh Jesus, I'm gonna come — " He tried to pull back from Jed's mouth, but the cowboy held on tight, his lips moving up and down on Charles' cock as if his life depended on it.

"Jed!" Charles's shuddering cry echoed through the stillness of the night as his orgasm took over all his senses. He barely heard the muffled response of encouragement from Jed. For a split second, he teetered on the edge of delirium, his chest heaved, the sound of his gasping breaths thrummed in his head. His hips bucked and twisted, caught in the throes of the exquisite pleasure that now racked his body. He wanted to shout with joy, but all he could manage was a reedy whimper as he climaxed, his semen jetting into Jed's mouth.

Jed's hands stroked and caressed Charles' smooth torso, his fingers nipping at the small, hard nipples. He released Charles' cock then kissed the glistening head before sliding up to reach his lips. He ran his tongue over the plump lower lip, allowing Charles to taste himself. Charles met Jed's glowing eyes and smiled. He stroked Jed's faintly bristled jaw and kissed the cleft on his chin.

"You are one hot cowboy," he whispered.

Jed kissed the tip of Charles' nose and smiled. "I like you, Charles."

"And I like you, Jed." His hand skimmed the length of Jed's hard torso 'til he found that even harder prize. "Time I took care of Little Jed," he teased, his hand enclosing the hot thickness of Jed's cock. "Correction — there's nothing little down there."

Jed smiled shyly. "I'd like to fuck you, Charles."

Charles looked up at Jed through slightly hooded, teasing eyes. "I think that can be arranged. But first..." He scooted down until he was eye-level with Jed's crotch. "This beautiful cock needs some attention."

Jed lay on his back as Charles went down on him, a hand grasping the base of his cock, warm lips touching the aching swollen head. His breath caught in his throat at the sensation of Charles' tongue dipping into the slit, lapping up the pre-cum he knew he'd been leaking ever since their first kiss and the first feel of Charles' lithe body against his.

He groaned softly, his body shuddering as Charles' lips slid down the length of his erection. Raising his head slightly, he studied Charles' body in the filtered light the moon overhead provided. Slim and lightly muscled with smooth skin that felt like silk under Jed's calloused hands, the sensuous sight filled him with a deep and undeniable yearning to possess Charles and make him his own. Crazy thoughts and surely only because of the amazing things Charles was doing down there. Jed groaned again, louder this time, the heat and friction from Charles' tongue scouring Jed's rock-hard shaft becoming almost unbearable.

Jed placed a hand on either side of Charles' body and moved him so he was kneeling astride Jed, his delectable ass only a few inches from Jed's eager mouth. Jed leant forward, his abs tightening with the effort, until his lips touched the cleft between Charles' butt cheeks. His hands kneaded and massaged the twin globes of flesh, parting them to make way for his reaching tongue. The puckered hole quivered as he probed at it with the tip of his tongue. A muffled moan escaped Charles, and Jed felt him quicken his strokes, sucking on Jed's cock with long vigorous slides and licks. Jed pushed his way inside Charles, his tongue swirling beyond the smaller man's yielded resistance, his hands gliding over the taut muscles that flanked the sides of Charles' torso.

"Want you now," Jed said, easing away from Charles' demanding mouth. Charles stayed motionless as Jed positioned himself behind him, then remembering, he fumbled inside his slacks back pocket and hand the foil wrapper to Jed. Jed ripped the foil open with his teeth then sheathed himself, noting that the condom was lubricated. He grasped Charles' slim hips, pulling him closer. With one long finger, he probed Charles' opening, made slick with his saliva, ran his finger lightly over it, circling it. He heard Charles breathing, fast, excited, full of anticipation. He slipped his finger inside, working his way around the hole, stretching with a gentle pressure before pushing his finger all the way inside. Charles moaned, and the sound inflamed Jed's senses, knowing he'd touched Charles' sweet spot. His other hand reached for Charles' cock and found it, hard and erect. Gently, he pulled out of Charles, replacing his finger with his cock head. He pushed slowly forward, his throbbing shaft entering the hot core of the man whose body now trembled under him, opening to him until Jed was balls deep inside him. Charles reared up, and Jed wrapped his arms around him, holding him pressed close to his chest. He laved Charles' neck with his lips, nipped at his ear lobes, his fingers caressed and teased Charles' nipples. Charles writhed against him, pushing against his impalement, his neck arching, seeking Jed's lips with his own.

"Dear God," Jed breathed into Charles' mouth. "Swear I've never felt anything like this before." His mouth crushed Charles', their tongues meshing, tussling, sending fiery sparks of excitement through both their bodies. Jed's hips thrust upward, driving his cock even deeper inside Charles, sliding back and forth inside Charles' heat. They were both moaning now, oblivious to anything but each other. Jed wanted this to never end. He didn't even want to come, because then it would be over, and he didn't want it to be over. He wanted to go on holding this sweet man in his arms forever.

But the rhythm Charles had initiated between them, along with the incredible friction of their combined bodies, took over. His thrusts became quicker, rougher, and Charles pushed back, urging him on. He grasped Charles' erection, pumping it in time to his rapid strokes. His orgasm gathered in his balls, and his breathing rasped in his chest. Every nerve ending came alive in his body. Every muscle stiffened with the onslaught of his climax. A deep wrenching groan was torn from his lips as he exploded into the latex that separated Charles' flesh from his. Showers of bright pinpoints of light burst behind his eyelids. He heard Charles cry out then felt him shudder against him, and a warm gush fill his hand as Charles came. Their bodies seemed to sink into one another as Charles collapsed against him, turning his head to gaze into Jed's eyes.

Jed kissed him tenderly. "You are truly something else, Charlie — sorry, I mean Charles."

Charles smiled. "I think you've earned the right to call me anything you like — and Charlie's just fine." He nuzzled the soft skin under Jed's Adam's apple. "That was..." he paused and clenched his ass muscles around Jed's still-erect cock. "...or rather, *is* amazing."

"Yes, it is. Thank you, Charlie."

Charles chuckled. "You said that like it's never going to happen again."

"Oh, it'll happen again. We've got all night, and you don't leave 'til Sunday evening." He moved back slightly. "But I'm gettin' a cramp in my ass in this position, so what say we stretch out and clean up a little. I've still got a fistful of you right here…"

"Good idea," Charles said, lifting himself off Jed. "You got a towel or something handy?"

"There's a rag in the corner there. Best I can do."

Charles reached for it and handed it to Jed who used it to wipe up.

"You got another of these?" Jed asked as he carefully peeled the used condom from his semi-hard penis.

"Sorry, no. That was it. Where d'you suppose the nearest pharmacy is?"

Jed laughed. "Nowhere 'round here, unfortunately. " His eyes narrowed slyly. "But back in my room —"

"Aha —" Charles snuggled back into Jed's arms, and the two of them laid back down on the Jeep's floor, Charles resting his head on Jed's chest, one finger tracing the outline of each ab muscle. "You must work out a lot to keep in such good shape."

"Not so much. Ranch work keeps me pretty fit though." He felt Charles' biceps. "You're in good shape, too. You have a sweet little body — and a sweet little ass."

"Thank Royce for that. He insists I go to the gym with him three times a week."

"You like living in LA?"

"Love it. I can't imagine living anywhere else to be honest — but this little getaway has been nice. More than nice."

"I'd like to think you'll come up to the Double R more often now."

"Are you inviting me?"

"Well, it's not my place to invite you, but I was thinkin'... Only, maybe it's too early to be askin' you stuff, but we could meet, say in Sacramento for a weekend, or something."

Charles raised his head to look at Jed. "You mean that?"

"'Course, I mean it. I wouldn't say it just for the sake of sayin' it."

"How about next weekend?"

Jed's chuckle from deep in his chest sent a thrill through Charles. "That's what I like about you. You know what you want, and you're not afraid to ask for it."

"So it's a go for next weekend?"

"Tomorrow, I'll talk to Parker. If he says I can have the weekend off, it's a go."

"What if I talk to Parker?'

"Uh-uh, Charlie. I'm new on the job, and I don't want Parker thinkin' he has to grant me favours just 'cause I'm itchin' to be with you."

"Itchin' to be with me," Charles murmured. "I think that's the most romantic thing anyone has ever said to me."

"You're makin' fun of me now."

"No, I'm not," Charles exclaimed, poking Jed in the ribs. "I'm actually very flattered."

Jed grabbed Charles' poking finger and placed it between his lips, sucking on it slowly for a second or two then he said, "Leave it with me then, and I'll take care of it."

Charles smiled and pressed himself deeper into Jed's embrace. He tried to remember the last time he'd felt this *good* in any man's arms. Yes, he'd had his share of hot men, some positively stunning in their own way, but none of them had made him *hunger* for them the way he now hungered for Jed. As he lay there in the shelter of Jed's arms, Charles was considering something he thought he never would – a long-distance romance. He'd seen so many of those fail, yet Royce and Parker had made it work for them, and Los Angeles wasn't *that* far from Sacramento. The idea of Jed and himself in some cosy hotel room, on a king-size bed, had a definite appeal.

If we could have such fantastic sex in the back of a Jeep, parked on some dark country road, think of what we could do on a real bed or in a big shower…

The thought of Jed's superb body, slick with soapy water, was enough to recharge Charles' libido, and make him very hungry again. He let his hand roam over Jed's smooth torso until his fingers brushed over Jed's flaccid but thick cock. It stirred under his touch, and he heard Jed's soft chuckle.

"I was just goin' to ask you what you were thinking about," he said, covering Charles' hand with his own. "And now I guess I know."

"You've made me insatiable for you," Charles murmured, kissing Jed's chest.

"Well then, let's get back to the ranch, and I'll sneak you into my room."

"Reminds me of my college days. Never thought I'd be sneaking into a guy's room at almost thirty years old!"

Jed sat up, taking Charles with him. "You're that old?"

"Hey!"

Jed laughed. "Just kidding. I'm just a year behind you." He kissed Charles soundly on the mouth. "Okay, let's get dressed and head back. Guess you could use a shower, too."

"Only if you do," Charles said, slightly stunned by the effect Jed's kiss had on him. "Personally, I like the scent of a man after sex."

Jed grinned. "You know just what to say to get me goin'." He took Charles' hand and placed it over his burgeoning cock. "See what I mean?" he whispered. "We better get going 'fore I forget we don't have another condom."

"Right. Just tell me you have a major supply in your room, 'cause you're going to need more than just one or two!"

Jed's hearty laughter warmed Charles' heart, and for the first time in as long as he could remember, the thought of returning to Los Angeles didn't bring him any pleasure at all.

Chapter Seven

Royce rolled over onto his stomach and flung an arm out to start his morning cuddle, and hopefully more, with Parker. He encountered an empty space.

"Damn," he muttered, sitting up and swiping at the blond hair that hung over his forehead. "Up already?" He glanced at his watch. *Seven. Oh well, that's late as far as Parker's concerned.*

He wondered if Charles was up. Royce couldn't wait to hear how his little ride in the Jeep with Jed had turned out. Must have been good. He hadn't heard him come up to his room. *Maybe they spent the night in the Jeep.* He chuckled at the thought as he got out of bed and padded into the bathroom. After he'd splashed his face with water, he pulled on a tee and a pair of shorts then went in search of his friend. Giving the door a gentle knock, he peeked into Charles' room.

"Hey, sleepy head," he said to the mound under the comforter. "You going to stay there all day?"

A deep groan was followed by, "Go away, I just got here."

Royce grinned. "Okay, come down and get some coffee when you're ready."

"Wait." Another groan. "I'll get up. Sleep seems to have escaped me for some reason."

"Guilty conscience?" Royce chuckled as a dishevelled Charles appeared from under the comforter.

"Nothing to be guilty about," he growled then gave Royce a smug look. "Unless having mad passionate sex four times with a cowboy would make you guilt-ridden."

"Wow, I'm impressed," Royce said, sitting on the edge of the bed.

"So am I." Charles gazed at him through bleary but happy eyes. "It was incredible, Royce. *He's* incredible."

"Are you in love?"

"I don't fall in love, Royce, you know that. Love 'em and leave 'em is my motto." He paused and closed his eyes. "At least, it used to be." He opened his eyes and gazed at Royce again as he added, "He is such a nice guy. No ego or attitude, though after last night, and this morning, he has every right to have both."

"So you'll be sorry to leave the Double R tonight?"

"Sorry, like you're sorry. " Charles smiled gently. "You're always a bear Mondays after a weekend with Parker. I think I'll miss Jed the cowboy on Monday."

"You can always come back with me anytime, you know that."

"Thanks. He did mention a weekend together in Sacramento."

"Fantastic! When?"

"Uh, this weekend, if Parker will let him take it off."

"I'll make sure he does."

"No, Royce. Jed was insistent we don't put pressure on Parker just because we're friends. He doesn't want to start looking for favours from the foreman after only two days on the job."

"Oh, okay. Well, are you coming downstairs for coffee? I need one even more now after your revelations."

Charles threw back the covers and ran, naked, into the bathroom. "I'll be right there," he yelled.

Royce smiled to himself as he left the guest room. *Charles might say he doesn't fall in love,* he thought, *but I've never seen that wistful look on his face before when he's been talking about the guys he's been with. Could be my friend Charles may have fallen and just doesn't know it yet.*

* * * *

Jed was out in the corral with Parker looking at two new horses when one of the hands yelled, "Hey, Jed, there's a phone ringing in your room."

He clapped his back pocket. "My cell. Forgot to pick it up."

"You wanna go get it?" Parker asked.

"No, I'll check my voice mail later."

"So what d'you think?" Parker asked, directing Jed's attention back to the horses.

"They're both beauties — the bay in particular."

"Okay, guess she's yours then."

"Huh?"

"The boss said for you to take your pick. Long as you're here at the Double R, she's yours."

"Wow, that sure is nice of Mr. Chandler." Jed looked thunderstruck. "He always this good to his hands?"

"Yep. Long as you do a good job and don't cause trouble, he's the best boss you'll ever find." Parker nudged Jed's arm. "Well, go saddle her up and take her for a ride. Hope she takes to you. By the way—" A small grin creased Parker's lips. "You have a good time last night?"

"Uh...yeah. That Charlie's a different kind of guy."

"Still callin' him Charlie?"

"Yeah, he said it was okay if I did."

"Huh." Parker's grin got wider. "You guys *must* have a good time last night."

The back of Jed's neck was red as he walked away to get his saddle. Parker chuckled to himself. "Yes sir, must have been real good last night."

* * * *

Jed was unpacking his saddle when he remembered his cell phone had been ringing earlier. He picked it up—one message.

"Hi, Jed—"

Jed sat down quickly on the bed as a familiar voice filled his ear. *Brett.*

"Just wanted you to know I miss you, buddy. Things aren't working out too good for Alan 'n me. Wondered if you'd give me a call when you have the time. Sure do miss you."

Jed stared at his cell phone for several minutes after the message ended. Brett missed him. He felt a surge of excitement mixed with apprehension. Things weren't going good with Alan, but what did that mean exactly? Brett had split up with him before, they'd gotten back together and flaunted their happiness in Jed's face—who was to say that wouldn't happen again?

Still, Brett had sounded blue. It wouldn't hurt to call him and commiserate some. He punched in Brett's number, his heart pounding as he listened to the ring tone.

"Jed, thanks for calling back."

"Hi, Brett. You all right?"

"No, not really. Alan's being a royal pain in the ass. Whining at me day and night about living here in Cattle Valley. Wants us both to go back to San Francisco. Jed, I don't want to leave here. I just wish things were the way they used to be—you and me, you know?"

Jed took a deep breath then asked quietly, "You're saying you want me back?"

"Yeah. I guess that's what I'm saying. I miss you, buddy, really miss you."

"Have you told Alan you're not going to San Francisco with him?"

"Not exactly. He's liable to make a scene in front of everyone, you know, like he does."

Jed frowned. Yes, he knew—knew very well what Alan was capable of, and he'd never been able to understand why Brett had put up with it, ever.

"What is it you want me to do, Brett?" he asked.

"It feels so good just talkin' to you, Jed."

"It's good talkin' to you too, but—what is it you're plannin' to do?"

"I don't know." Brett's voice held a plaintive tone Jed didn't recognise. He sounded indecisive, unsure, not like Brett at all. He must really be in a bad way. That fuckin' Alan.

"Brett, I just started here at the Double R. I can't just up and leave at a moment's notice."

"I know, I know." Brett fell silent then in a rush said, "Well, it sure was good talkin' to you, Mr. Harper, sir. We'll get right on it." The line went dead.

"What the hell?" Jed closed his phone and slipped it into his back pocket. He could only imagine that Alan had come into the office, making Brett pretend he was talking to a client. Jesus, what a mess. He knew Alan wouldn't let up on Brett 'til he got what he wanted. He'd nag and withhold sex until he wore Brett down—that was his way—and Brett was a damn fool to put up with it. Still, Jed couldn't just ignore what had obviously been a cry for help. He'd give it a day or two then call Brett back. Maybe he'd have come to some decision by then.

He picked up his saddle and headed outside to the corral then stopped dead in his tracks when he saw Parker had been joined by Royce—and Charlie. So, what the hell was he going to tell the man when he mentioned the weekend in Sacramento? *Forget it—there's a chance I can get back with my old boyfriend?* No, he couldn't say that, but he couldn't in all good conscience string Charlie along thinking they were embarking on some kind of relationship. Yeah, their time together had been incredible, and in between their bouts of fantastic sex, they'd talked and talked, about how easy it would be to get together—they'd even talked about Jed going to LA, a city he'd never even thought of visiting. But now?

Charles smiled at him as he started walking over to the corral. "'Mornin' Charlie, Royce…"

"Parker was just showing us the horse you picked," Royce said.

"Yeah, that's so good of your dad." Jed heaved his saddle up onto the top bar of the corral fence. "That bay is a beauty."

"Maybe we could go riding again today," Charles exclaimed, getting a surprised look from Royce.

"Well, I got some things for Jed to take care of," Parker said.

Charles pouted. "But it's Sunday!"

The other men laughed. "There's no Sundays on a ranch, Charlie," Jed told him. "There's always stuff to do."

"Don't worry, Charles." Royce put an arm round his friend. "They'll be done by lunchtime then we can kick back together before we have to leave for the airport."

"What time's your plane?" Jed asked.

"Six-thirty." Charles gave him a small smile. "Are you coming with us?"

"Yeah, Jed," Parker said. "Be company for me on the road back."

"Okay." Jed was happy to be included. Seeing Charlie in the bright light of day after their very full night of sex didn't diminish his affection or his attraction for the man one bit. If they'd been alone he'd have been all over him in a flash. He really wanted to taste those sweet lips one more time.

Royce grinned at Parker as he sensed the energy between Jed and Charles. "Hey, Parker, before you whisk Jed away, you wanna show me what you were talking about up at the house?"

"What was that exactly?"

"You know—" Royce did an eye roll.

"Oh, right—that. Yeah Jed, be back in a few."

Charles and Jed watched with some amusement as Royce hustled Parker back to the house. "I think in their own subtle way they're giving us time to talk," Charles said, laughing quietly.

"Yeah." Jed's smile was gentle as he met Charles' eyes. "How are you this morning?"

"Never felt better—despite the lack of sleep. You?"

"Great. Charlie…" Jed broke eye contact with Charles. "There's something I need to tell you."

"Oh, oh." Charles tried for flippancy. "You're married with five kids."

"No. I—"

"You're working for the FBI."

"No, Charlie I—"

"I know, you're—"

"*Charlie.*"

"Sorry. I just have a feeling I'm not going to like what you're about to tell me."

Jed sighed and kicked at one of the corral railings. "Before I came out here, I was seeing someone. He broke up with me when his ex came back into his life."

Charles stared at him wide-eyed. "What was he? Nuts?"

Jed smiled. "Thanks for that, but no, not nuts, just still crazy about the guy who ditched him and went to live in San Francisco."

"And now?"

"He just called me a little while ago. Said things weren't goin' too good, and he missed me, and—"

"And you're ready to take him back." Charles shrugged. "Well, hey, don't worry about hurting my feelings. As the song goes, 'It was great fun, but it was just one of those things'."

Jed stared hard at him. "Is that all it was Charlie?"

"What else do you want me to say, Jed? It was incredible, fantastic, something I'll remember all my life?" Charles took a step back, his eyes glistening. "Yes, it was all of those things, Jed, but it was just one night. I'll get over it, forget it, and so will you."

"Charlie—"

"I know, I know, you feel bad. I understand that, but we have no claims on each other's lives. How could we after only one night together?"

A wry smile twisted Jed's lips. "Two, really."

"One you can barely remember." Charles held out his hand. "Goodbye, Jed. I won't expect you to come to the airport with us."

Jed took Charles' hand and looked around the ranch yard. "Everybody's busy. Come to the barn with me so we can say goodbye properly."

"I don't think so." Charles pulled his hand from Jed's grip. "I wish you all the best, Jed, whatever you do."

Jed watched Charles walk away, half of him wanting to run after him, pick him up and carry him off to the barn, the other half realising this was for the best and that Charles was making it easy for him. No tantrums, no accusations, just a clean cut and goodbye—it had just been so cold, so final. A long sigh escaped his lips as he pulled his tackle off the top bar of the corral and went in to saddle up the bay. The horse stood still as he slung the saddle across her back. He stroked the bay's black as coal mane and petted her muzzle.

"There girl, you and me are gonna be good friends—if you don't mind havin' a damn fool for a friend."

Chapter Eight

One month later

Royce scanned the crowds hurrying the airport security gates at LAX airport, his eyes searching for the cowboy hat Parker was never without. When he finally caught sight of him, his head of crisp black curls was unadorned. Parker was holding his hat in his hand as he talked with a little old lady in a wheelchair.

Always the gentleman, Royce thought with a smile. He watched as Parker handed the lady her purse. *She must've dropped it.*

"Parker!"

Parker looked up and waved at Royce then after quick goodbye to the old lady he pushed his way through the barrier and hurried over to where Royce stood with open arms.

"Oh, it's so good to see you," Royce exclaimed.

"Good to see you too, darlin'." Parker leant back to jam his hat on his head and gave Royce his slow grin. "You look good enough to eat."

Royce chuckled. "And you shall, later. Got some news," he added as Parker shouldered his carryon and the two of them strode towards the exit.

"Oh yeah? Good, I hope."

"Good and bad," Royce replied. "Good 'cause I've persuaded one of the partners to open an office in Sacramento with yours truly in charge. Should be finalised in about six months."

Parker beamed at him. "That's terrific, Royce. Yippee— no more airports!"

"Right, but the bad news is, Charles isn't coming with me."

"Damn," Parker muttered. "He's still hurtin'?"

"Hurting and mad. Jed called him the other night."

"Oh, boy. Well, that was my doin'. Jed said he'd called Charles several times but hadn't left messages after the first one. I kinda thought if they talked they could work things out."

"According to Charles," Royce said, "there is nothing to work out. Anyway, he didn't return Jed's call."

Parker sighed. "But Jed didn't go back to that other guy. He told me he was a fool to even consider it. He really likes Charles, Royce." They paused to let several cars go then crossed to the parking garage.

"Crazy thing is, I'm sure Charles still likes Jed. He just feels that if Jed was sincere he'd have shown up by now instead of letting so much time go by without a word, then a phone call out of the blue that was supposed to make everything right."

"Jed's not good at this kind of thing," Parker remarked. "Big as he is, I think he's scared Charles would kick him in the pants if he showed up at his door." He squeezed Royce's arm. "Remember, it took your daddy's accident to get us back together. So many times I wanted to call you, and I just couldn't bring myself to do it."

"You cowboys." Royce shook his head. "Stubborn, macho pride—" He fell silent as they got into a crowded elevator. He smiled at Parker over the head of an elderly Chinese man being berated by his diminutive wife.

"Poor guy," Parker remarked as they stepped off the elevator. "Wonder what *he* did."

"So, how's Jed doing at the Double R? Are you and Dad happy with him?

"Sure. I feel confident enough to leave him in charge while I'm here with you. He's a good man. I'm gonna put my two cents in when I see Charles."

"Good luck with that." Royce levelled his remote at his BMW and opened the trunk. "He's not really receptive to all things Jed right now," he added, watching Parker stow his bag in the trunk. They got in the car and cruised out towards Interstate 415.

"You know…" Parker turned in his seat so he could look at Royce. "Jeez, Royce, but you are one beautiful man. Don't go getting stuck in any traffic jams, or you might have to pull over so I can jump your bones in the car."

Royce laughed. "You are such a romantic, Parker Jones. But thanks, I think you're pretty hot, too."

Parker leaned over so he could kiss Royce's cheek. "Anyway, that wasn't what I was going to say. You just kinda took my breath away. What I was going to say was the way Jed tells it, Charles didn't even get mad when he told him about the guy in Cattle Valley. He just said somethin' about it bein' only one night and he had no claim on him whatsoever."

Royce nodded. "That's Charles all over. Leave with your head held high. Thing is, Parker, Charles has never been in a long term relationship with any man. He'll tell you, love 'em and leave 'em is his motto. But I just get the feeling this time he was falling for Jed, and that's what's making it so hard for him to come to terms with this. Not to be overly melodramatic about it, but I think he was ready to open his heart, and he had it crushed."

"He said that?"

"No, he'd never admit it, not even to me — probably not to himself."

"Damn, Royce, we gotta do somethin' about this."

"Like what, Parker? You're dealing with two stubborn souls here, and they're nearly four hundred miles apart on top of that. It's not like we can engineer them bumping into one another in the supermarket."

"I didn't say it was goin' to be a piece of cake, but we have to think of a way."

Royce turned to smile at him. "Okay, deal. We can think of ways to reunite Charles and Jed anytime you're not jumping my bones."

"Hmm…" Parker stroked Royce's thigh thoughtfully. "That's not giving us a lot of time to think."

The phone was ringing when they rushed into Royce's apartment, both of them already pulling at each other's clothes.

"You wanna answer that?" Parker panted, unzipping Royce's fly.

"Absolutely not." Royce grabbed the back of Parker's head and pulled him in for a long, loaded kiss. "It can go to voice mail," he added when they came up for air. He pulled off Parker's shirt, exposing the tightly muscled body he adored. His hands slid below Parker's loosened belt to caress his firm smooth butt. Royce's breath shuddered in his chest. "Oh, babe, missed you so much."

"Missed you..." Parker's reply was lost as Royce took his lips again, their hands pulling at what few clothes they still had on. Parker half carried Royce into the bedroom then they both toppled onto the bed, arms, legs and lips locked together in a passionate embrace.

The phone rang again.

"Shit," Royce mumbled.

"Maybe it's important," Parker said, sitting up.

"If it's not, I'll kill whoever it is." Royce rolled to the side of the bed and grabbed the phone. "Hello?"

"Hi, it's me."

"Oh, hi Charles. Something wrong?"

"No, just wanted to welcome Parker to LA. He is here, isn't he?"

"Yes, he's here. I was just welcoming him myself, as a matter of fact."

"Oh, shit, I'm sorry, Royce. Jesus, you'd think I'd know better that that. I'll get off the line. Tell Parker hello and say I'm sorry."

"Tell him yourself." He handed Parker the phone.

"Hi, Charles." Parker spooned Royce as he talked, his hard cock buried in the cleft between Royce's butt cheeks.

"Sorry, Parker. Just wanted to say hello and welcome."

"Thanks. We'll be seeing you later?"

"Yes, Royce asked me over for dinner — but if you guys would rather stay in bed, I'll understand."

"Naw. Royce will have worn me out by dinnertime. You come on over."

"Okay. See you later then. Bye."

"Bye, Charles." Parker reached over Royce to put the phone on the nightstand. "He's lonesome," he murmured in Royce's ear.

Royce sighed. "Yes, he is, and I feel guilty about being so happy to have you, right here, holding me, your cock so nice and hard against my ass — and there's no way I could wear you out by dinnertime!" He turned in Parker's arms and nibbled on the full lower lip he loved so much. Parker rolled over onto his back holding Royce pressed hard against him.

"We'll talk about Charles later," he said, returning Royce's kiss. "Remember? Only when I'm not jumpin' your bones!"

* * * *

The doorbell rang just as Parker and Royce were stepping out of the shower.

"That'll be Charles," Royce grunted, towelling himself off quickly. "I'll just throw on a pair of shorts and let him in — you however, get dressed, Mister. I don't want him getting all fired up looking at your too-tempting body."

Parker chuckled as Royce kissed him. "You have a monk's robe I can wear?"

"No way. We all know what those randy monks can get up to!" Royce slipped into a pair of shorts, grabbed a T-shirt then ran to open the door. He was pleased to see Charles looking fresh and smiley, not the sourpuss he'd been at work recently. He dragged Charles inside and gave him a big kiss on the cheek.

"Where's Romeo?" Charles asked, hugging Royce then handing him a bottle of cabernet. "You untie him yet?"

"Just." Royce squeezed himself into his T-shirt. "We've been at it until the doorbell rang."

"Good for you. I'll have a scotch rocks – a big one. Don't worry, I took a cab over."

"Charles…"

"Yes, Royce?"

The two men stared at each other for a few moments then Royce shrugged. "Nothing." He went behind the bar to fix Charles his drink. "Parker will be out in a minute."

"I hope Jed's not going to come through that door with him. Oh wait–" He laughed dryly. "You're not into three-ways, are you?"

Royce sighed. "Hardly – besides Jed is acting-foreman when Parker's not there."

"Oh."

Royce slid Charles's drink in front of him. "Disappointed?"

"Of course not."

Royce studied Charles for a moment. "I think you are."

"You're delusional." Charles took a long swig of his drink. "Royce, we've been here before. I am not pining for Jed Miller. The guy was hot, is hot, but just as I thought in the beginning, before we got in the sack together, he's heavy with baggage, and I'm just not that into him enough to share the load." He took another long swig of his scotch. "Furthermore, if he was as interested in me as you and Parker seem to think he is, he could have called me a lot sooner than the other night."

"You make him nervous," Royce said, grinning.

"Who told you that?" Charles scoffed.

"Parker."

"Now what'd I do?" Parker chose that moment to appear in the living room.

Charles' jaw dropped slightly. "Wow, I've never seen you in shorts before. You have the cutest hairy legs, Parker."

"Well, hello to you, too, Charles." Parker chuckled and gave him a hug. "I thought I heard my name bein' taken in vain."

"Royce said you told him I made Jed nervous."

"You do," Parker said, smiling at Royce who'd handed him a cold beer.

"How in hell could I make a six feet four cowboy with shoulders as wide as Texas nervous?"

"Don't ask me," Parker replied laughing, "but you can come across as a bit of a ball-buster at times."

Charles affected mock indignation. "*Me*? I like balls too much to go around busting them."

Royce couldn't resist. "How about Jed's balls?'

"Royce, you really are becoming quite the filth-monger." Charles smiled impishly. "Okay, if you must know, they were beauties—and everything else that went with them. Satisfied?"

"And still you won't give him the time of day?"

"That's right. Now, can we talk about something else? The price of tea in China? The state of the economy? Anything, other than Cowboy Jed!"

* * * *

When Charles returned to his apartment later that night, his answering machine light was flashing in the darkness of the living room. Somehow, before he pressed the 'play' button, he knew it would be Jed's voice he would hear. And there it was, that low-pitched seductive huskiness that sent a visceral thrill straight to his cock as he listened.

How could that man not know his own power to enthral with just a few carefully chosen words?

"Hi Charlie — do I still have the right to call you Charlie? I sure hope so, and I hope you'll return my call one of these days. In case you threw it away, here's my cell number..."

It's a plot, isn't it? Charles mused as he deleted the message. He'd bet anything that Parker had told Jed the three of them were having dinner together. Probably said he'd 'put in a good word'! Charles smiled. *Friends.* Well meaning, but sometimes they just couldn't see they were wasting their time. He walked over to the bar, poured himself a nightcap then lay on the couch and flipped on the TV.

"Wouldn't you fucking know it," he groaned as Randolph Scott galloped across the screen being chased by whooping Indians. *Well, Randy's certainly no substitute for Jed*, he thought, quickly changing the channel. After surfing through the whole cable repertoire and still finding nothing to watch, he switched off the TV and lay staring up at the ceiling, and thinking, as he had done every night since his return from the Double R, about Jed. There was no way he would ever admit it, not even to Royce, but he missed the tall cowboy, more than he'd ever thought possible.

For almost a month now, he'd thought about Jed almost every waking moment. Sometimes, even despite his workload at the law offices he found his mind straying to that night when he and Jed had made love over and over in the cowboy's small but pleasant room at the Double R ranch. It should have felt raunchy and seedy, the two of them, still almost strangers, devouring each other like the end of the world was just 'round the corner. But it hadn't felt wrong at the time, nor did it now. It had been wonderful, exhilarating, deeply sensual, and when Charles was completely honest with himself, the best sex he'd ever had—bar none. The most completed he'd ever felt.

He'd been so tempted to return Jed's call the other night, and now again tonight, hearing that sexy voice it had almost been too much. A vision of Jed's rugged, good looks and hot body swam before Charles' eyes, and he closed them to hold on to the sensual image and to imagine that he could feel Jed's soft lips on his, his strong arms enfold him, hear his husky whispered words , his lips pressed to Charles' ear—

"Cut it out!" Charles yelled, sitting up so fast, he slopped his drink on his shirt. "Damn it." He jumped to his feet and pulled off his shirt, rubbing at his damp chest and fuming for allowing himself to become maudlin and fantasise over something—some*one*—he couldn't have. "Get a grip, Charles," he muttered. "Drink up and go to bed. Tomorrow is another day—*right*."

Chapter Nine

"Okay, I've had enough of this."

Jed gave Parker a startled look as his foreman poked him on the arm and glared at him from under his wide-brimmed hat.

"'Scuse me? What'd I do?"

"Nothin' — and that's the problem, Jed."

"But I've been workin' my tail off every day since I started here at the Double R," Jed said in protest. "Boss Chandler, just the other day said he was real happy with me workin' here."

"I'm not talkin' about your work, Jed." Parker heaved a loud sigh. "Okay, here's the deal, Jed. You're a great worker, and I'm really glad you're here, but you've gotta do something about that unhappy face of yours. At least, try smilin' once in a while, will you?"

"I'm sorry, I didn't know that was part of the job."

"Well, it is. No, oh hell—no it's not, but I sure as heck hate seeing you go around so damned *morose* when I know what'll fix it."

"What'll fix it?'

"Don't act like you don't know what I'm talkin' about."

"Parker, I—"

"I know you want to tell me to mind my own damn business," Parker interrupted, "but I'm under orders, you see, and it's taken me three days since I've been back from LA to get this far with it. Royce is going to call me again tonight, and if I tell him *again* I still haven't broached the subject of you and Charles, he's gonna whoop my ass when I see him next weekend."

Jed's stony expression dissolved as he shouted with laughter. "Boss, I think I might pay good money to see that!"

"Yeah, well it ain't gonna happen," Parker growled. "'Cause you are goin' to get on a plane to LA and go see the guy you've been hankerin' for, for over a month now."

"Parker, I can't do that. He'll probably take one look at me and slam the door in my face."

"Then you just have to knock the door down."

"Parker—"

"Listen to me Jed. Royce and me had a difference of opinion some time back, and we didn't talk to one another for close to a year. It was the worst year of my life, and I cussed myself out a thousand times for not havin' the gumption to do what I'm tellin' you to do. Now I'm being deadly serious when I say that Charles will not slam the door in your face. I can assure you of that."

"Maybe I should call him first."

"And give him the chance to say no, if he even answers your call?" Parker shook his head. "Look, Royce and I have talked about this, and he convinced me this is the way you should tackle Charles. Be there, and let him see what he's been missing. Those are Royce's words, not mine, you understand — that last part."

Jed grinned at him. "Royce has you really well trained, hasn't he?"

"Huh. He likes to think so, and I let him get away with it, now and then. So, what d'you say, Jed? We can manage without you for a of days, and there's a flight out of Sacramento later this afternoon. Royce'll meet you at LAX."

"This afternoon? Shit, I'd like to think about this."

"Don't. If you do, you'll find a million reasons for not going, and you will live to regret it, buddy. Believe me."

Jed sighed and hunched his wide shoulders as if still unsure. "If he tells me to go to hell—"

"Take the chance, Jed." Parker chuckled and slapped Jed's arm. "He's just a little guy."

Jed smiled. "Yeah, but he sure doesn't act like a little guy!"

* * * *

Several hours later, Jed stood on the sidewalk outside Charles' apartment, holding the bouquet of flowers Royce had insisted they stop to buy on the way. Royce smiled encouragingly from his idling BMW.

"Go on, Jed," he urged. "Third floor, apartment three-o-seven. It's at the far end of the building. He's home — I checked."

Jed nodded and tried to smile. "Thanks, Royce. Maybe you could wait a few minutes in case he kicks me out."

Royce chuckled. "He won't, but if it makes you feel better, I'll hang around for ten minutes or so. And Jed — good luck." He watched the tall cowboy disappear inside the main doors to the apartment building. He crossed his fingers. "Don't fuck this up, Charles," he murmured as he pulled away from the kerb. He'd circle the block once, just to make sure…

Jed took a deep breath and rapped on the door marked three-o-seven. He stood for some time waiting then he knocked again.

"I'm coming!"

Hell, he sounds irritated. Like I need to get him mad before *he opens the door.*

The door swung open, and Jed and Charles stood staring at one another for a long moment, Charles' light grey eyes widening with surprise — or was it shock? Jed wondered. Charles wore a little pair of shorts and was towelling his hair. He'd obviously just got out of the shower. Was he going out? Jed thrust the bouquet of flowers at Charles. He cleared his throat and managed to croak, "Hello, Charlie…s, *Charles.*"

Charles took the flowers, and Jed gave a small sigh of relief. Surely, he wouldn't slam the door in his face after accepting the flowers?

"Come in." Charles stepped back and opened the door wider. "This is a surprise, Jed. Why didn't you call to say you were coming?"

"Are you going out?"

"No." He eyed the overnight bag hanging from Jed's shoulder. "Where are you staying?"

"Uh, with Royce."

"Oh? Funny he didn't mention that to me."

"Uh, right. About that..." Jed decided to go for broke. "Hell, Charles, I've been meaning to do this for the past month. I've called you so many times, but—"

"You've called me twice, Jed."

"Twice that I've left a message. So many other times I just hung up when I heard the answering machine. But you didn't return my calls, so Royce and Parker—"

"Royce and Parker, eh?" Charles smiled wryly. "I might have known. They are just so determined to put you and me back in each other's arms. It's really quite amusing."

"Amusing?" Jed frowned. He let his overnight bag slip from his shoulder and drop to the floor. "I don't think it's funny. I think it's real nice of them to care about us, to see that I was festerin' over not seein' you or hearin' from you. I was a fool to tell you about that call from Brett. All it did was get your dander up, and in the end, it came to nothing—my choice, Charles. If you hadn't acted so damned cold about it, this would never have happened!"

Charles bristled. "You're saying this is all my fault?"

"No, I'm not sayin' any such thing," Jed said, sighing. "There you go, getting feisty before you hear what I have to say."

Charles eyes softened as he gazed at Jed's earnest expression. "Go on then, I'm listening."

"What I'm trying to say, Charlie, I mean Charles, is I have missed you something terrible. All I do is think about that great time we had together, how you felt in my arms. How great you kissed—" He hesitated for a moment, then said quietly, "You look so nice, Charles—even nicer than I remembered, if that's possible."

Charles suddenly realised he was still clutching the bouquet of flowers. He walked over to the kitchen counter and laid them down. "Thank you for these," he said. He looked across the room to where Jed stood looking back at him, uncertainty in his eyes. *God, but he is so beautiful,* Charles thought. *Such a beautiful guy — such a good guy. Am I being a total fool for not jumping into his arms and telling him I've missed him too, and this is just the greatest thing — seeing him standing here in my apartment? Tell him now, dummy —*

"Can I get you something to drink?"

"Uh, yeah, sure. You have a beer?"

Charles opened the refrigerator and brought out a beer bottle. "Light, okay?"

"It's swell, thanks."

Charles poured himself a shot of scotch and downed it in one swallow. He ran a hand through his hair, realising for the first time it was still damp, and he was still only wearing a little pair of shorts. *Nothing like being obvious.*

"Oh, look at me," he said forcing a laugh. "I better throw on some more clothes."

"You look just perfect to me," Jed said.

"I do?"

"Yes, you do. Perfect in every way, Charlie, I mean —"

"Jed —"

"Hell!" Jed came around the counter into the kitchen and pulled Charles into his arms. His mouth crushed Charles' lips, the whimper of protest Charles had begun, dying in his throat as Jed's size, his strength, his man-scent overwhelmed his senses, and he was returning Jed's kiss with all the fervour he could muster.

"Charlie, Charlie," Jed crooned, "I have missed you so much. Tell me you've missed me too."

"I have, you big lug —" Charles almost didn't recognise his own voice — it sounded like he was going to start sobbing at any moment. "I've missed you every damned day, and I've hated you and myself for being so stupid and stubborn, and I kept asking myself how could I feel this way after only knowing you for that brief time. I've never felt this way before, Jed—never. I even missed hearing you call me Charlie."

"Good, that's good, Charlie," Jed said, holding Charles even tighter. "'Cause I've never felt this way about anyone either."

"What about that guy in Cattle Valley?"

"Forget him." Jed placed his big hand on Charles' butt and pulled him into his crotch, hard. "I realised almost right away that it would be the dumbest thing I could do if I went back there just 'cause he was lonesome." He kissed the tip of Charles' nose. "I've been lonesome too, Charlie. For you."

Now, Charles did feel like crying. "All this time wasted, Jed—a whole month when I could have been right here in your arms and feeling your luscious lips on mine, instead of *festering* just like you were and too stupid do anything about it." He wound his arms around Jed's neck and let himself be lifted into the taller man's arms.

"That's better," Jed said, his lips brushing Charles'. "I was gettin' a crick in my neck bendin' over to kiss you."

"Maybe we should do this horizontally," Charles suggested. "Let me show you the bedroom."

"Point the way," Jed said, not putting Charles down.

"Door to the right of the fireplace," Charles murmured, his lips pressed to Jed's neck.

With a few long strides, Jed was in the bedroom. He laid Charles down on top of the bed then started ripping off his clothes. Charles watched with a hungry impatience as Jed stripped, baring his beautiful body, his every movement one of fluid grace. He even managed to look good as he balanced on one foot to pull off his boots.

Enjoying Charles' eyes on him, he unbuckled his belt, unbuttoned the fly of his jeans, pulled them slowly down over his hips, taking his briefs at the same time. Charles gasped as Jed's erection sprang free. Long and thick and hard, it curved upward to his navel, proud and vital, and ready for Charles' attention. He knelt on the bed facing Jed as the cowboy crawled towards him, the light of desire in his eyes, a small sly smile playing on his lips.

Jed reached for him, drawing Charles' smaller body into the warmth of his embrace, their mouths meeting in a kiss that had both of them moaning as the sensuous intensity of it took control of their senses.

"Jesus, Charlie," Jed gasped. "You feel so good, even more incredible than I remembered all these past nights when I lay in my bed and thought of what we'd shared. This is like a dream come true for me, Charlie. You here, in my arms again."

Charles silenced him with another kiss, and Jed lowered him onto the comforter, lying over him, covering his body with his own, his slick, throbbing cock sliding over Charles' pulsing erection. Charles gazed up into Jed's hazel eyes and felt his heart turn over. As sensuous as this moment was, what pierced him to the heart was Jed's sincerity, and in that split second of time, he knew he had fallen in love. The realisation of it brought a soft moan to his lips, and he pressed himself ever deeper in Jed's arms, winding his legs around Jed's thighs, clinging to him as if his life depended on him. And in a way it did, for now he was ready to give it all up for this man, go anywhere he asked, do anything he wanted him to do. For a moment, he was terrified, for he had never before felt this way in his entire life.

And what if Jed didn't feel the same way?

As if he intuited Charles' sudden apprehension, Jed tightened his arms about him, holding him safe and conveying without words the love he felt for him. Charles seemed to melt into Jed, his hands caressing Jed's thrilling body, bringing them both to an intimacy neither man had ever experienced before. Jed's kisses were rough and demanding, his lips and tongue scoured Charles' mouth, his throat, his chest, lingering over each nipple, biting gently, causing Charles to cry out in ecstasy, his body writhing under Jed's hot, moist kisses.

Jed grasped Charles' rigid cock at the base.

"Beautiful, Charlie," he whispered, before engulfing it with the heat of his mouth, his tongue licking up and down the underside of Charles' hard shaft, then sweeping round the head, gathering up the pre-cum that oozed from the slit.

"You taste good, Charlie," he mumbled before devouring the pulsing flesh again.

"Need to taste you, too," Charles said, tugging on Jed's wide shoulders, and the cowboy shifted his long, lean body, presenting his thick, throbbing cock to Charles' lust-filled gaze. His fingers reached to stroke it, tantalisingly gentle at first then as Jed shuddered under his teasing touch, Charles grasped it firmly, pumping it between his lips, his tongue savouring the tangy, salty essence that spilled from it.

"Mmm..." Charles' spontaneous hum of appreciation sent a vibration from the head of Jed's cock to his balls. His hips bucked, driving his erection deeper in Charles' mouth. Charles struggled to take all of it—there was just so much—biggest by far he'd ever seen, never mind had inside him—and oh, but that's where he wanted Jed now, deep inside him, filling him completely, making him his own. Charles gave a final suck then released Jed's cock and reached for the lube and a condom.

"Want you to fuck me, Jed. Need you inside me where you belong."

Jed raised his head from Charles' crotch and grinned at him. "How'd you know that's just what I was thinkin'?" They kissed, their moist lips tasting of one another. "This is the best night of my life, Charlie. I love being here with you."

Charles' eyes glistened as he met Jed's hazel gaze. Surely, it was too soon to tell him how he felt, and yet, the sincerity in Jed's eyes, the soft smile on his lips, made Charles feel that his declaration of love would not be too hasty. Still, better wait. He tore the foil wrapper open and stretched the latex sheath over Jed's hard, thick shaft.

"Tight fit," he muttered, using some lube to help. "Best get you the larger size, next time."

"I've been told that before," Jed said, without a trace of ego.

"I'm sure you have," Charles chuckled.

"I'm glad you said that."

"What?" Charles smiled at him. "That you need a bigger size?"

"No, that there'll be a next time."

Charles kissed Jed's lips tenderly. "A next time, and a next time."

"*Charlie*—" Jed's voice caught in his throat, and he crushed Charles in his arms. "Oh, Charlie…"

Charles fell back, pulling Jed with him. His legs encircled Jed's waist, and he raised his hips giving Jed clear access to his tight but eager opening. Jed's breath escaped his lips in a long sigh as he pushed forward, the head of his cock slipping past Charles' brief resistance and burying itself in the silken heat beyond. A long groan was wrenched from Charles before the fiery pain deep inside him gave way to the ecstasy he knew would follow. He wrapped his arms around Jed's neck, bringing their mouths together in a kiss that consumed them both and took Charles to what he would later swear was an out of the body experience. *Never* had any man been able to transport him like this. He gasped as Jed pulled back then thrust forward, pulled back again then forward, the head of his cock gliding over Charles' prostate with each delicious pass, sending sensational sparks and jolts of exquisite pleasure coursing through his blood. Charles matched Jed's rhythm, bearing down on the rock-hard cock that impaled him as it was driven deeper inside him with every powerful push of Jed's hips.

Jed gripped Charles' erection in is big hand, pumping it to the movement of their bodies. Their eyes locked on one another, and Charles felt the slow roil of his impending orgasm build in his balls.

"Jed," he choked clinging to the cowboy's wide shoulders. "Oh, dear God, Jed —"

"Yeah, come for me, Charlie," Jed gasped. A drop of the sweat that had beaded on his forehead dropped onto Charles' lips. Charles licked at it and smiled into Jed's eyes. His body stiffened then shuddered as he climaxed, his semen spraying over his chest, his chin, even under Jed's jaw.

"Beautiful," Jed crooned, licking at the warm cum before taking Charles' lips in one hot kiss after another. Charles felt the muscles bunch across Jed's shoulders, his body vibrating as his orgasm overwhelmed him. A long, low, guttural cry escaped Jed as he came, sending his seed jetting into the condom buried deep inside Charles. He held on tight to Jed until his body calmed, and they both settled in the shelter of each other's arms.

"Can I tell you now, Charlie?" Jed whispered, his lips touching Charles'.

"Tell me what?'

"That I love you, with all my heart and soul."

"Jed, I…"

"Is it too soon?" Jed looked at him with worried eyes. "Am I bein' too hasty for you?"

Charles brushed Jed's lips with his own. "Yes, it's probably too soon, but—" He laid a finger on Jed's slightly open mouth as he started to protest. "But, too soon or not, I love you too, Jed."

"You mean it?" Jed's eyes searched Charles'. "You really mean it?"

"I really mean it, Jed. I love you."

Jed's arms tightened around Charles, and he buried his face against Charles' neck. "You have made me the happiest man in the whole wide world."

Charles chuckled and kissed Jed's ear. "Let's hope you're still saying that after twenty years or so." At one time in his life, Charles could never have imagined making that statement, but just then it had seemed the most natural thing to say. "On second thoughts, let's make that forty years."

Epilogue

Six months later

Charles and Royce sat together in the stands under the broiling sun at Reno's annual Gay Rodeo. Royce kept nudging Charles since his friend tended to sit with his eyes closed half the time, especially when Jed was in the arena either bronco riding or steer roping.

"Sorry, my nerves just can't take this," Charles hissed after Royce had poked him in the ribs a half dozen times.

"But you're going to miss Parker's best bout," Royce protested. "He's won this competition three years in a row. You have to cheer him on today."

"I'll cheer with my eyes closed."

"How're you gonna do that?"

"When you cheer, I'll cheer!"

"Open your damned eyes, Charles, or I'll tell Jed you didn't see him do one thing out there—and you know, he'll be crushed."

Charles opened his eyes wide and glared at Royce. "You wouldn't!"

Royce chuckled. "Oh yes, I would." He looked over Charles' shoulder. "Oh, look who's here."

Charles looked up at the tall figure approaching their seats. "Don't you dare tell him," he muttered under his breath.

Jed slid in beside them and put an arm around Charles. "You enjoyin' yourself, Charlie?"

"Oh, yes. It's exciting," Charles enthused, trying not to feel like a traitor.

"Expect you got rattled some when that steer trampled me," Jed said, squeezing Charles. "But don't worry," he added, after kissing Charles on the cheek, "he didn't hit anything vital. Got a few bruises, but I'm still in working order."

"Good." Charles smiled into Jed's eyes. No way was he going to tell him he would have passed out if he'd actually seen him being trampled on. "You were the best out there."

"No, that honour goes to Parker. And look, here he comes now! Go, Parker—yippee!"

Both Jed and Royce jumped to their feet, screaming their lungs out for Parker. Charles had no choice but to follow suit. He had to keep his eyes open as Jed thumped him on the shoulder and yelled in his ear as Parker came flying out of the holding pen astride a horse that was behaving as if it were mad.

How could Royce stand this? Charles wondered, cringeing at the sight of the horse and Parker bouncing around the arena as if there were springs attached to the bronco's hooves. Any minute, he expected to see Parker fly through the air and break his neck on the hard-packed ground—and yet, Charles had to admit, there was something totally awesome about watching man and beast fight it out—exciting enough to be a complete turn on, especially since Jed now had his arm around Charles' waist, his hard body pressed against him as he jumped up and down.

"Go, Parker! Ride 'em cowboy!" Charles heard himself screaming at the top of his voice and Royce grabbed him round the neck as the buzzer went, signalling that Parker had exceeded the time limit and was once again champion. The three of them hugged and kissed and waved as Parker waved to the cheering crowd.

"He's the best!" Royce crowed, blowing kisses at his boyfriend.

Charles winked at Jed. "Well now, that's kind of debatable."

* * * *

Later, as the four friends drove the two hour trip back to Sacramento, Royce said, "Oh guys, Parker and I want to show you where we'll be living when we open the new office."

Charles and Jed, sitting in the backseat, stopped necking long enough to pay attention.

"Jed's actually seen it," Parker remarked. "Remember Jed, that first day you were on the Double R, we went into town for provisions and stopped to look at some acreage on the way back?"

"I remember."

"My dad bought it for Parker and me," Royce said proudly. "We're going to build our own ranch house there, and Parker's going to raise horses and open up a dude ranch for gays."

"So you got yourself a promotion, Jed," Parker said, "if you want it. Foreman at the Double R when I leave. I already talked to Aaron, and he's good with it."

"That's real nice of you, Parker." Jed grinned at them. "I could use the extra cash—Charlie's got expensive tastes."

Charles raised an eyebrow. "I have *good* taste. I chose you, didn't I?"

Jed chuckled. "Can't argue with that."

"There's lots of room on the land, guys," Royce told them. "If you want to build yourselves a house near ours—we could be neighbours!"

"Thanks, Royce, that's sweet of you," Charles said, "but I'm still a city boy at heart. Jed and I looked at a townhouse in Sacramento last week, and I think we might go that route. It's only an hour from the ranch."

"Not much of a commute," Jed added.

"And we can spend weekends together, once you get your house built." Charles sighed contentedly. "Only another month or so, and we'll be in the new office. I can't wait!"

* * * *

After Royce and Parker had dropped them off at their hotel in Sacramento, Charles and Jed lost no time in getting out of their clothes and into the shower. As they stood under the hot spray, Charles leant back into Jed's embrace and wriggled his butt against Jed's hard cock.

"I think that life's pretty much perfect, right now," he murmured, turning his head for Jed's kiss.

"You think?"

Charles raised an eyebrow. "You don't ?"

Jed chuckled from deep in his chest, his soapy hands caressing Charles' chest. "More than perfect, Charlie. Like you once said — idyllic."

"Yes." Charles turned in Jed's arms and wrapped his arms around his lover's neck, pulling him down into a long and languorous kiss. "And now, I know what you meant that night when you asked me if I'd ever been in love," he whispered against Jed's lips. "Now I know what it's like to want to wake up every morning with you by my side, to live with you, and *for* you only. I love you, Jed."

"Love you too, Charlie," Jed murmured. "With all my heart and soul."

About the Author

J.P. Bowie was born in Scotland and toured British theatres in numerous musical shows including Stephen Sondheim's Company. Emigrated to the States and worked in Las Vegas, Nevada for the magicians Siegfried and Roy as their Head of Wardrobe at the Mirage Hotel. Currently living in Henderson, Nevada.

J.P. Bowie loves to hear from readers. You can find her contact information, website details and author profile page at http://www.total-e-bound.com.

Total-E-Bound Publishing

www.total-e-bound.com

Take a look at our exciting range of literagasmic™
erotic romance titles and discover pure quality
at Total-E-Bound.